short fiction and poetry by

Gabriella Goliger
Sharon Hawkins
Nadine McInnis
Sandra Nicholls
Susan Zettell

edited by Rita Donovan

BuschekBooks

Canadian Cataloguing in Publication Data

Main entry under title:
    Quintet

Short fiction and poems.
ISBN 0-9699904-5-6

   1. Mothers and daughters—Literary collections.
2. Mothers and sons—Literary collections. 3. Canadian
literature (English)—20th century. I. Donovan, Rita, 1955-
II. Goliger, Gabriella, 1949-

PS8237.M64Q55 1998   C810.8'0355   C98-900785-5
PR9194.52.M64Q55 1998

Quintet
Printed and bound in Canada by Hignell Printing Limited, Winnipeg, Manitoba

BuschekBooks
acknowledges the support of
the Canada Council for the Arts for
its publications

BuschekBooks
P.O. Box 74053
35 Beechwood Avenue
Ottawa, Ontario K1M 2H9

THE CANADA COUNCIL   LE CONSEIL DES ART
FOR THE ARTS   DU CANADA
SINCE 1957   DEPUIS 1957

E-mail:buschek.books@sympatico.ca
Web Site: http://www3.sympatico.ca/buschek.books/home.html

John Buschek, Editor

Table of Contents

4

Wanderers

BY GABRIELLA GOLIGER

Rachel dips her foot in and out of the pool of sunshine on the wall above her bed and wonders what to do. It's Saturday morning, a shining day and a thousand green hands wave from the maple tree outside. The choices are to join her mother on the long walk to the Steinbergs store or take her chances in the laneway, which might be full of kids later on, the scuffle of feet chasing after rubber balls. But what if everyone's away on errands or holed up with Saturday morning cartoons?

There's no point in trying to tag along with her brother Avi. Just once, she'd love to sit with him in a ditch by the side of the road at Dorval Airport, watching planes take off and land, hearing his voice above the roar of engines, but hell could freeze over before that would happen.

The door swings open, and Rachel's mother bursts in, in bare feet and nightgown, makes a bee-line for the balcony that opens off Rachel's room. Hannah grabs the handle of the balcony door that sticks in its jamb. She yanks. The glass panes rattle. Gusts of cool summer breeze blow through the room. Hands on the railing, Hannah sucks in early morning air, the only air, she says, that's clean and not yet blown out of other peoples' mouths or dirtied by traffic.

In another moment she's at Rachel's bedside inclining her face.

"Where's my kiss," she whispers, her voice choked.

The signs are bad. Rachel sees this right away. The red-rimmed watery eyes, the grabbing-on-to-you stare. She looks like she's spent the last hour locked up in the bathroom again with the taps on full blast and one tiny, nasty word or shrug could send her back. Still, Rachel's mind is made up. The laneway beckons. A fast, wild game of handball is what she wants. She plants a smack on the cheek that leans down to her, wriggles backwards and folds her arms across her chest.

"I'm going to play with friends. I'm not coming shopping."

"You don't want to come with me?" Her mother's eyes dart around the room, searching, as if something's gone missing. She sinks down onto the edge of the bed. Then she recovers.

"Of course you're coming. It will do you good, a proper walk in the fresh air. The last time I came home to find you howling under my bedcovers."

This was true. Rachel had found no one to play with, returned home to the empty apartment where the silence in each room mocked her like a friend turned mean. Each piece of furniture had become a stranger — couch, dining room table, the radio on her parents' dresser, the cuckoo clock with its dull brass pendulum — all cold and hard, and despite hating herself for it, she did indeed cry, first a low whimpering into the pillows on her parents' bed, then full-throated baby wails. She bawled into the empty grey space under the bedspread until Hannah walked in with her bulging string shopping bags. Ashamed and relieved, Rachel promised herself that it would never happen again.

"I'll be OK this time, don't worry." Rachel is restless to be dressed and outside, away from the smell of the sleep-rumpled bed. No sound comes from Avi's room next door. Maybe he's already pedalling his way across town to the airport, his eyes peeled for a streak of silver in the sky.

"Your father..." Hannah starts, looks away. "Your father will be working late." Rachel remembers now, dimly as in a dream, the sounds of voices hitting against each other, one low, measured, steady as a saw rasping into wood, the other shrill and fluttering. Rachel sees the stiff-ness in her mother's back, how she needs a hand to touch and stroke her right in the dip where neck meets shoulders.

"I could help you unpack groceries when you come home. I'll play on the street so I see you coming."

But Hannah doesn't answer. She sits with legs crossed, hands laced around her thick knee, rocking slightly. Pale skin peeks from a gap in her nightgown where a button has come undone. All Hannah's dresses and nightgowns are the same style with a long row of buttons

6

up the front. She likes clothes she can slip in and out of without a struggle.

"When we lived on the kibbutz in Israel," she often says, "we wore shorts and shirts and sandals and no one ever thought about it. Who had time or money for anything else?"

In clothing stores, when the salesladies try to show her something new, a dress she would have to pull over her head or that zips up the back, Hannah's mouth twists.

"Oh no, it's not for me," she says in a small apologetic voice that makes Rachel walk away to another section of the store. But even her usual dresses don't work quite right for Hannah. A button, around the middle or near her knees, comes undone. A loop of hem hangs down. Rachel's father is forever pointing with his finger at the open place.

"There, there! Can't you see?" Ernst mutters as Hannah fumbles. "For God sakes, the way you run around."

Hannah slumps forward onto the bed beside Rachel, hands clenched, knuckles pressed against her cheek. Her back is arched up, stiff, quivering, awkward as if pushing against a weight that is pressing down on her, that can't possibly be resisted for very long. Rachel wishes this hump that is her mother would fall limp and still beside her. She stares through the milky sheers over the window at the side wall of the apartment building across from their own.

It's a good wall for handball. A long expanse of brick with few windows to get in the way. Rachel's old rubber ball is cracked and pockmarked, its spongy insides exposed. It flies off at crazy angles when she smacks it against the brick with the palm of her hand. She longs for a brand new one, for a smooth red, white and blue surface, rubber that is firm in her hand and that bounces straight up high.

The hump strains, quivers, shakes. Rachel's stomach tightens. She can't bear it. She wants to scream and flail her arms but her hands do something quite different. They become like the white-gloved Mickey Mouse hands in the cartoon that detach themselves from Mickey's body to play piano all by themselves. Her hands reach out, one rests on Hannah's shoulder, the other strokes the back of Hannah's head, lightly, lightly tickles the greyish scalp under the thick black hair, cut in a straight line along her neck. She is amazed at what her fingertips know, the delicate movements they invent and the magic that flows through them. The hump softens, sinks down. Her mother sighs between clenched teeth.

Now there's no longer any question of what to do. Rachel knows she will trot by her mother's side with a string bag in her hand, up the long street and through the woods behind the university. Certainty clamps down like a hand on Rachel's shoulder, bringing with it a dull grey calm, a kind of relief.

Avi is dressed, standing on the balcony, scanning the sky. From just behind their building, it seems, comes the roar of engines. Then a grey pencil shape arrows up from the horizon.

"TCA Super Constellation on its way to Winnipeg." Avi's voice purrs with certainty. It's impossible to tell when he is bee-essing, pretending to have X-ray vision like Superman. The grey pencil thins, lightens to a silver streak trailing white smoke.

"You can't see the name on the plane."

"Of course not. So what." Cool and offhand. His face is tilted away from her, but his eyes flick sideways. The triumphant accusations die in her throat. Her dumb-girl self is about to be exposed.

"I know it's a Super Constellation by the three-pronged shape of the tail and the sound of the engine. That's the plane TCA's using for long-haul flights. And it's nine-o-five," Avi says with a glance at his wristwatch. "TCA Montreal to Winnipeg departs at nine."

Avi has memorized the schedules off the signboards at the airport. He can reel off the names — BOAC, Lufthansa, Swissair, PanAm — their departure times and arrivals, the number of miles they will travel to reach their destinations and the number of horses that would cover the sky if you could convert horsepower literally. He knows, too, what keeps an airplane from falling out of the sky, the invisible forces of air and earth.

Sometimes, when he squints at the sky and intones the names and numbers, he says, "I'm making an educated guess," but this is when Rachel is most impressed. It is what he becomes when he gazes upwards like this, his eyes narrowed with concentration, his voice strong, deep, unstoppable as a radio announcer's. The whole world spinning, humming, ready for take off, inside him.

8

When it's time to leave, Hannah stands by the front door with the handle of her purse between her teeth, both hands deep in its belly. She's making sure she has everything — keys, money, kerchief, shopping net, mailbox key, "*Um Gotteswill*" the mailbox key is missing. It should be in the zippered side pocket, but it's not to be found and so she rushes back into the bedroom, rips open the top dresser drawer, hands rummaging among the underwear.

"I just had it a second ago," she wails.

Rachel has an inkling of where it must be. On the kitchen table, looped over the salt shaker for safe-keeping, but she continues to linger by the door, glued to the spot. The frenzy of departure is giddy-making — like watching a pie-throwing scene on the "I Love Lucy" show. Rachel wants to laugh out loud as she watches her mother tear at knots of balled up nylons. She also wants to flop down in weariness onto the hallway floor.

Hannah races down the corridor into the kitchen. A yell of triumph. The key is found, attached to its merry strip of red ribbon and exactly where Hannah laid it down. A last check of everything and they're out the door, down the three flights of stairs to the street below.

Halfway down the street, though, Hannah stops dead, utters a gasp. She begins, as Rachel knew she would, to fret once more. The possibilities of all that can go wrong between the opening and the closing of the apartment door bear down on her. Is the stove really off? The toaster unplugged, the bathroom and kitchen sink taps really shut? Hannah doesn't trust her own hands or eyes. She is only satisfied after Rachel runs back for a final, final check.

"Everything's fine!" she shrieks in triumph from halfway down the block.

"Thank God, Thank God."

They step forward together into the early summer breeze.

The Steinbergs on Côte des Neiges is about a mile from their house, a short ride by streetcar, but Hannah prefers to walk and not just because of the money either. Hannah hates everything fast and electric. The blue sparks that dance on the streetcar rod make her shiver, and, when she does ride, the rocking motion of the car makes her face go white and clammy.

"I should have been born in another time," she says. "In my mother's time. The world was so much nicer with only horses and buggies."

Hannah can remember a fairy-tale life of long ago. She once rode with her parents in a black coach over cobbled streets. And before electric lights, there were lanterns. A man came along with a long pole to light the gas that hummed near the schoolroom ceiling, making Hannah so nice and sleepy.

Even better than riding coaches, Hannah says, is to walk where you need to on your own two feet. This is one subject her parents agree on — the pleasures of walking. On fine Sundays, when Ernst doesn't have to work, the whole family sets out across the Mountain and the Christian cemeteries to the lookout that hangs over the city like a balcony. Rachel loves when the four of them go together. Four is the perfect number. Four wheels to a car. Four legs on a table. The number that holds things up.

The walk over the Mountain, Ernst and Hannah say, is a real excursion, European style, not a little circle around the block which is what Canadians call a walk. The green of Mount Royal with the spidery cross in the distance reminds them of the forests, castles, the school outings back home. The whole class would take the tram to the end of the line and they would march all day long, drunk with fresh air and freedom. They were wandering, but they weren't lost like Goldilocks in the forest. In Europe you could walk off in any direction and eventually end up somewhere — a village or a barnyard where a farmer's wife might offer you milk fresh from the cow. Try that in Canada, Ernst likes to predict, and you'll get stuck in the bush with a thousand blackflies up your nose. In Europe, there were wandering songs that everyone knew — like Christmas carols — and everyone sang them to get into the swing and sway of forward motion.

Hannah begins humming to herself as she and Rachel walk together down the long sun-warmed street. Under her breath at first, she half whistles, half sings, until her voice, rich and low, wells up. "Freut euch des lebens." Rejoice in life. Rachel chimes in here and there on the notes that are easy to reach. Since they are walking briskly they can do this — sing without being noticed by the woman in the yellow housecoat and pink sponge curlers who is sweeping her front steps or by the fat man with his feet up on the balcony railing. They pass by as if they were on a train, seeing everything but invisible to everyone on the outside.

"Tell about the time you ran away," Rachel says.

"Ran away?" Hannah looks down puzzled. "Where should I run?"

"You know. When you ran away from home. Across the border. When you walked for three days all alone."

"Oh that. When I went to the training school. But I didn't run away, I just left. It was still easy to leave Germany at that time. I walked through the *Riesengeberge*, the mountains near our town by myself until I got to the Czech border. Someone had told me about a Herr and Frau Schatz who ran an agricultural school for young people, preparing them to be pioneers in Palestine. At first they didn't want to take me. There I was scratched and dirty on Herr Schatz's front porch and he stares at my swollen feet through his old-fashioned monocle and shakes his head, 'We need big strong boys here, not girls. You'd be devoured by the Palestine fevers in a week.' But we get talking. He asks me about my town, my family, and suddenly he slaps his hand to his forehead. 'Your father's in the Lessing Lodge? Why didn't you say so?' And that was that. I was in. Can you believe it? I am still here on this earth, and you are here, and your brother too, because my father was in the same lodge with Herr Schatz."

Her voice, which has been light and singsong as if she were reading a fairytale, now trails off into a mutter. She is far away again in her dark cloud, the immense dark cloud of another time, before Rachel was born. That time is like a puzzle whose pieces usually fit together in a snap. There was a war. Hitler came like Pharaoh to kill all the Jews, but a few Jews escaped over the sea and rebuilt their land out of nothing. They came out of their crowded alleys into the brilliant light of the Land. They threw away their canes and monocles, dug their hands into the hot sand and flowers burst forth where their fingers had ploughed. Many were killed, but some were saved. The chosen. But sometimes it's as if pieces from a completely different puzzle got mixed in by mistake and nothing fits. Patches of colour with no shape to them.

They arrive at a busy corner where the light is changing from green to yellow. Hannah's hand grabs Rachel's in a tight grip although they've both already come to a full stop on the curb. As the cars roll by,

Hannah tells Rachel to take shallow breaths, so that the stink of the car gas doesn't enter her lungs.

Rachel doesn't know what a lodge is and suspects she still wouldn't understand the story if she did. Nor can she quite believe it about her mother walking through mountains all alone, although she sees quite clearly a grown-up girl, slim and tanned, with muscled arms and sturdy legs. The girl on the first page of the photo album, looking up in surprise. Oh yes, she sees this girl with the little bundle on her back and one arm swinging free. She strides along the road, bold and confident.

"Why did you go alone? Why didn't Dad go with you?"

"But that was before I met your father. Don't you remember? I was on an excursion in the mountains with the *Wandervögel*, the youth group. Someone talked about the agricultural school, about learning to pitch hay and milk cows. And I just decided it was for me. I decided to go right away. I left next day from the youth hostel."

"But what did your parents say? Did they let you go?" This story about walking away with nothing, no goodbyes, is just too wonderful, yet Hannah speaks as if it were the simple and ordinary truth. Rachel remembers the time when she herself stayed out after dusk in the woods across the street to find the house in an uproar when she came home. Her parents had called the police.

"Oh, I suppose I wrote home when I got to the training school. Those were the times. Everyone on the move." Hannah shakes her head.

Rachel could listen to it again and again, the story about the girl on her solitary journey. A girl who turned her mind inside out like a pillow case, shook out any lingering timidity and filled herself with certainty and purpose. What did she eat? Where did she sleep? Were Hitler's men hiding in the bushes by the side of the road? Rachel wants to know more, but Hannah never seems to remember any of that. She shakes her head again. So long ago. What she tells about is the joy of walking in the mountains in a time before highways. The pine-scented wind. The distant cowbells. The cathedral of treetops. The holy stillness of the woods.

They emerge from Steinbergs weighed down by string bags of groceries. Hannah clutches the ones with the heavy stuff — sacks of potatoes, onions, cans of Spam, the gallon jug of Javex, Old Dutch cleanser. Rachel twirls the bag that holds bread and oatmeal, and although it's not heavy now, she knows it will get worse and worse.

"Let's take the streetcar Mama, just this time." Hannah looks at her sideways as the streetcar swings around the corner and lumbers towards them. It is crammed full of Saturday shoppers whose heads roll forward and back with the motion of the car. The ride would bring them home in five minutes flat and Rachel would have new transfers to add to her collection. She has a shoebox full. They once belonged to Avi before he gave up on streetcars to concentrate on planes.

"You'll only get sick. It's not so far to walk," Hannah says.

The streetcar drifts away in a shower of blue sparks. The street it leaves behind is long and straight, a monotony of buildings, an endless line of telephone poles and sidewalk slabs. Her legs turn stiff and stubborn. They will never get her home.

"Look, let's pretend we only have to go to the next telephone pole," says Hannah. "Come, it's not so far."

In a few steps they are at the pole.

"Now just to the next one," Hannah says.

"To the next one," Rachel yells, dashing forward.

One by one, poles come to meet them, poles are left behind. They are walking again with feet that know their business. Walking like breathing in a rhythm that takes over. One, two, one, two.

When they pass by the Catholic cemetery, Rachel and Hannah turn onto the shortcut, a path that winds through woods, sumach groves and a field of hip-high weeds where bees buzz and butterflies flit. On one side, tractors have been cutting a new road into the ground. The earth where the tractors rolled by is raw and mashed down.

The sky is a vast, watery blue, so far away that Rachel can't imagine how airplanes reach it so quickly. A few moments is all it takes and the plane is transformed from a lumbering metal elephant into a silver speck. High above now, a pinpoint of light pierces the blue, pulling behind it a long thread of white smoke. She blinks. The white thread breaks up into ragged patches like pieces of couch stuffing. Avi could make such patches connect up again in his mind into a straight line pointing across the oceans at a place called London or Paris. He could find his way in that endless blue. Rachel can't imagine ever in a million years being able to distinguish the voice of one engine from another or looking up at a pinpoint of light and calling it by name like an old friend.

A small cry tears the silence, stopping Rachel in her tracks. Hannah is a short way back on the path, stock still, bent over, the grocery bags scattered around her. Mouth open, she is peering into a tangle of leaves, staring as if she wants to pour herself into the spot. Rachel can't see anything at first except a bumblebee that knocks against Hannah's hip and zig zags away.

"There. Right there."

On a leathery leaf sits a black and orange butterfly. It's the same as dozens that Rachel saw flitting by them in the field, except this one has come to rest, its wings spread open, just quivering slightly.

"Do you see? So beautiful," Hannah whispers, squeezing her hands together. Rachel sees what Hannah means. The delicate pattern of segments and dots. The glow of orange against velvet black. But there is too much of something in Hannah's face. And the grocery bags shouldn't be lying like that, limp and exposed, so that anyone passing by could see how much they have to carry and all their things — the dented tins for five cents off, the Javex that Hannah uses for scrubbing the toilet.

Rachel tugs at her mother's sleeve but Hannah doesn't seem to hear. She stands, a lump, only her chest heaving in and out. The back of her neck is red and sweaty beneath the straight line of chopped off black hair. The cardigan tied by the arms around her waist and swaddling her broad hips is bunched up with burrs.

If some boys from Rachel's school were to come upon them now, Hannah wouldn't notice until they were all around them, sticking their tongues out of the sides of their mouths and making circling motions with their fingers around their heads.

Crazy. Crazy. Rachel feels the nasty words form on her lips. She wants to punch the heaving breast. She wants to fly down the path and never look back. But the look on Hannah's face. A breathless wonder that is almost like pain. An anguished rapture. Rachel drops her eyes, yet still sees her mother's look burning away into the back of her mind.

She takes hold of her mother's hand, the thick, swollen fingers with purple lines across the knuckles where the string bag cut. She feels the coolness of her own hand pass over to soothe the sweaty heat.

"Come on, Mama," she says. "Let's go."

Mother Tongue

BY GABRIELLA GOLIGER

I want her to tell me a story. One of those old German fairy tales that she loves so much and used to read to me as I lay in her bed, half sick with a cold, half faking it so that we could both stay home hulled in the feather comforter and make believe. Mother Holle. How did it go? A good girl and a bad girl. The good girl shook Mother Holle's feather-bed, made it snow on earth and a shower of gold coins rained down upon her. The bad girl disobeyed and was smothered in pitch.

It snowed outside as she read aloud. Fat, feathery snowflakes brushed against the window, danced down, drew us up into the spilled-milk sky.

Do you remember Mother Holle, I'll ask her just as soon as she wakes from the codeine-laced stupor that I am responsible for. Her head lolls back on the deck chair, her mouth gapes open and sucks in humid, lung-clogging Florida air. The sky beyond our screened lanai is the colour of pencil shading, dull and bright at the same time, it stabs the eyes. Everyone, everything, at Golden Gate Resort is quiet and hunkered down in the afternoon heat. Palm trees droop. The gecko on the railing has turned to wood.

She tried to read to me long after I was old enough to read for myself and had lost interest in her baby stories. I wanted stories in English — the language of the real world. *Little Women, Black Beauty, Nancy Drew*. And to read in my own bed, in the early morning before anyone else was up. She wanted to cuddle me against her pillow-soft breasts and read in her hushed, choked voice, almost crying the words: "What are you afraid of *mein Kind*? I am Mother Holle. I will do you no harm..." She turned the pages with trembling fingers. Age-softened, yellow-spotted pages with engravings of castles, tree bolls, porridge

16

pots, long-toothed witches. Later I had words to explain her. A *Romantik*, a German Romantik with a "k." Simmering with *Weltschmertz* and longing for a wild-wooded, pure-aired, pre-war, pre-industrial Germany that never was. What an absurd position, mother, what a quicksand to stand on for a Jew.

*

I wanted to get her a wheelchair. Just for a few days so that I could take her on excursions along the beach boardwalk and the mile-long path that circles Golden Gate Lake. So that she could look and listen and smell to her heart's content. The mint-cream sea, the misted sky, sandpipers, pelicans, hibiscus blooms in cocktail colours. Look and listen without pain for a change. But she won't allow it, prefers to walk on her own two swollen feet, rusty joints, ravaged knees, ground-down hips. She prefers to fight the searing arthritis that was supposed to dissolve in the Florida sun — that was my plan — but if anything it's become worse. Leaning on her walker she thumps down with her good leg, swings around the bad one that hangs down from her side like an anchor in mud. Long, muffled moan. Trickles of sweat on her seamed neck beneath the wide-brimmed hat and between the hunched shoulders. She inches forward.

If she were in a wheelchair I could push her around the lake in minutes and reach the little bridge she loves where she can look down and see turtles and ducks.

I shuffle beside her at her geriatric pace and plot my own battle against the pain-dragon. A warm bath. A nice rest on the lanai, legs elevated. Two extra strength Tylenol with codeine. Don't wait for the pain to get so bad that you'd need twice the recommended dosage to control it. I'll go to Publix myself for the groceries, spare her the crowded aisles, the blasts of icy air spewing out of vents and freezers.

But she insists on coming too. She staggers along, draped over the shopping cart, still dazed after a bad night's sleep and the morning's medication. She lingers at the produce department, eyes brightening over the heaps of melons, grapefruit, pineapples, mangoes. She weighs oranges in her palms, brings a yellow-skinned plum to her nose, leaves her shopping cart to lurch towards the strawberry sale while my back is turned. I see her stumble and catch herself just in time.

I steer her over to the bread department, last item on our list. Her eyes roam over shelves and shelves of choices — bagels, Italian bread, Polish rye, egg loaf, seven-grain — but none of them what she wants. None of them real bread. Her complexion is weary grey. She hangs over the cart.

"Mama, *komm' schon*. Come on. Just take something."

She prods a packaged loaf with her finger.

"*Wiederlich*! Clings to the roof of your mouth and gives you heartburn afterwards."

"Mama, I've had it."

The woman in the yellow tank top examining dinner rolls looks up and smirks, looks down again. Does she know German? Or is it just my universal, exasperated-daughter tone of voice?

"Don't talk so loud," I hiss, as I steer my mother towards the cash.

*

I have plans for our week together. I've come equipped. In the side pocket of my suitcase I've got a tape recorder and a five-pack of ninety-minute, low-noise tapes. I want to get her stories down once and for all. The ones she's told me a thousand times but which whirl around in my mind, names and dates and details mixed up. About my grandmother who died in the Spanish flu epidemic of 1919 leaving my mother motherless. About my grandfather and his two great passions — the Jewish Law and the German railway system. About the town she grew up in that no longer exists, a Polish city now, with everything that would be familiar to her, everything German expelled, three hundred years of history extinguished.

Stretched out on the deck chair, she sleeps the sleep of the battle-worn. At rest except for her tremor-ridden hand which dances a mazurka in her lap. The screened lanai enfolds us in bug-free shade.

She wakes, groggy and confused. Pain shoots back into her eyes.

"I saw a snake. There are snakes in the water."

"No, no mother. There are no snakes here."

She points the trembler. Golden Gate Lake lies still, ringed by clipped lawns and cream-coloured condos. A man-made lake with all the original swamp dug out of it.

"So many snakes. Long black snakes."

Golden Gate Resort is plastic-wrap pristine. No pests here, no cockroaches or ants even. Blasted every Tuesday by men in green overalls wielding spray guns. My stomach jumps. What's happened to her mind? Pain and medication have cut through the wires, leaving a stranger, a babbling stranger who once was my mother.

She presses her knuckles into her side, smiles up at me through a sigh and the abyss recedes. She is back.

"Where does it hurt, Mama?"

"Here. No here and here mostly." Her hands skim thighs, knees, rib-cage, belly. "I don't know. It moves."

"I'll get you some mint tea."

Put on the kettle. Find another cushion for her legs. Turn off the fan, she mustn't get chilled. Check the time for her next round of medication. Stow the suitcase with its tape recorder and tapes out of the way.

*

I will splash warm water over her legs to soothe aches lodged in bone. I will catch the pain devil by the tail. It leaps so quickly from joint to joint, limb to limb.

I grasp her under the arm, hold her steady, my naked mother. "Careful. Put your hand on the grab bar. That's it."

She lies back in the water, an old tired sack, gnarled feet, bloated belly. Yet despite the wrinkles and age spots, her skin is surprisingly soft and a fine, pale gold. I am awestruck still, uncovering her nakedness. How far we've come.

She shrieks as I sponge her sides.

"That tickles!"

She laughs, catches me with her laughter, hauls me along until we're both on this wild ride, unable to stop, doubled over. I fall onto the wet, tiled floor.

"Stop. Stop. I'll never get you out of that tub."

It comes to me later what she saw. Long, black, curved necks stretching out of the water. The anhinga, also known as the water turkey. A common Florida bird, not a snake.

*

We go by car to Knippels, the German delicatessen in an arcade of boutiques on Fifth Avenue.

"I have a surprise for you, Mama."

A smile dawns as she peers at the window pane, at Gothic script and painted dwarfs on the glass, red-capped, grinning, bearing between them a huge brown loaf on a board. More kitch in the display case beyond — glazed dough figures of Hansel and Gretel in front of a gingerbread witch's cottage, a doll-sized oven, miniature brooms.

I help her manoeuvre the walker around the glass door and into the store which is cool and smells like fresh-baked heaven. She eyes the shelves of crusty loaves and rolls.

"See Mama, this is where you can get real bread."

She leans towards a round black pumpernickel and sniffs. Then she notices the price.

"*Verruckt*, crazy," she says indicating the tall smiling man behind the counter. "Three-fifty, American, for this?"

"What do you want? It's a specialty shop."

"*Der Gauner*. Thief," she mutters.

"Shh. He'll understand."

"*Frisch*," says the storeowner. "Baked an hour ago." His smiling face looks like it too just came out of the oven. Brick-red cheeks. Small, black-currant eyes.

"How much for this?" she asks in her rough-hewn English.

"*Drei Dollar, neun und vierzig, bitte.*" Still smiling and inviting chat in their native tongue. Chat that would lead to embarrassing questions. ("Where in Germany are you from?" "When did you come to America?")

"Three forty-nine?" It's an accusation more than a question, and at his nod her hand begins to sink under the weight of the overpriced loaf. I toss exact change onto the counter and grab her arm.

The sweet aroma of warm bread fills the car. She stares at the dashboard, her face a battleground — anger, longing, suspicion, need.

We are surrounded by Germans. Young couples with children. Small groups of pensioners. Indistinguishable from the parade of other tourists with their bland, cheery faces and their Bermuda shorts, matching tops, sparkling white Nikes, except when they open their mouths, call out *"Jawohl,"* *"Guten Tag,"* jolting me with their strange-familiar utterances. This resort town on the Gulf Coast is a favourite destination for tour operators in Hamburg, Cologne, Berlin, all those rich cities well-padded in Deutchmarks which go so much further than our miserable Canadian dollars. They are not the majority of course. They are interspersed among the throngs of silver-haired snowbirds from northern states and Canada. Nevertheless, they are a presence. She drops her voice as we sit and chat on the boardwalk and the crowd streams by. Suddenly, big ears everywhere.

We have always spoken German together, laced with smatterings of Yiddish, Hebrew, English, my own bastardizations and our coinages and play words, endearments, quips and phrases repeated over decades. Our private, intimate language. Her mother tongue and mine, although I butcher the grammar and flounder for lack of grown-up words. My bedside-story, kitchen-table, toddler-self language, which I leave behind the moment I am out of her presence. Which I speak with no one else on earth. Ours is a country with a population of two.

It must have been a shock to me when I first realized that other people spoke German besides ourselves. I have been registering a series of mini-shocks ever since. I hid my understanding of their language when I met German speakers, preferring to let them approach me in English, a tongue that is cool, neutral, safe. I still do.

*

The check-out counter at Walmart's. A dark-haired woman about my own age behind me.

"Exyoose me," she says with a tentative smile, "Do you know vere zer iss a post office?"

A split second in which to decide whether to give her more than the stranger's answer. As always I give less, speaking slowly, so that she will understand, but allowing a fake American drawl to creep into my voice. Anything more is a minefield. Leads to false claims of common bonds. It's not her language I speak.

*

I am awkward in our mother tongue, but she is hilarious, emphatic, bold. Her lips part and out blows a flock of indignant sounds and crazy combinations. *"Abscheulich!" "Unerhört!" Es ist zum kotzen."*

She opens her mouth and out sails a song.

She used to sing in the morning in the kitchen before the rest of us were up. Hands sunk in dumpling dough — mashed potato, flour and egg — her deep voice boomed out old favourites, Schubert and Mozart and simple melodies with rocking-horse rhymes. *"Lieder... wieder...flieder...."*

It's been years now since she stopped singing, though she'll hum sometimes or whistle under her breath. A sighing sound like a dying wind.

*

Her English was uncooked dough in her mouth. It stained my childhood with foolish shame. I hid behind the cornflakes boxes as she asked questions of the smirking Steinbergs' boy, his face half turned away. "Pleece. How much iss ziss?" "Your epples, are zey goot?"

We spoke German together in the aisles, attracting a few over-the-shoulder glances but not the stares that her twisting and wrenching of English words would elicit. We chatted, incomprehensible and therefore invisible, our voices blending with the clatter of the cash register.

*

She used to have a ritual she called twilight hour. For a while, when I was growing up, she tried to draw me in. I came home from school in the afternoon and found the living room set up with armchairs pulled close to the big picture window, curtains pinned back for an unobstructed view of the maple tree, its bare branches spread against the grey winter sky. The coffee table proffered tea, chocolate mousse, tangerines. The radio poured forth Vivaldi. Something for each of the senses. Her Aunt Tilda had started the tradition, inviting her nieces to join her by the window overlooking gabled roofs and church spires. They sat in straight-backed chairs and recited poetry until the last of the daylight drained from the sky.

Mother wanted to read to me from her old book with the yellowed pages and the cracked spine that dropped dried glue crumbs on the table. The book wasn't from before the war — she had nothing at all from that time. She'd found it in an antiquarian bookstore on Mansfield Street. Poetry and tales from the Romantik era, printed in heavy gothic script that made me think of things massive and imprisoning — fortresses, dungeons, iron bars, marble tombs. She read in a singsong voice, emotion bubbling close to the surface, the beauty of the words threatening to push her over the edge into absurd exhaltation. I wanted to thrash and scream, yell bad words. Instead I did research. I scoured the reserve stacks at the public library for books on anti-semitism, German nationalism and discovered faint but perceptible arrows leading from *Sturm und Drang*, to Romantik, to Hitler.

"Open your eyes," I said.

A nasty epithet, a vile couplet, in the works of every one of your beloved authors.

"There was greatness as well," she said. "You can't dismiss a whole culture."

"Look here," I said, producing a verse by Wilhelm Busch, the humorist she quoted daily. "'See the Jew with crooked nose and crooked soul....'"

"And Shakespeare? And Dickens?"

And all those Germanophile Jews carted to the camps?

I switched on the standing lamp. It threw its glare around the room and blotted out the fading dusk.

*

23

The language of Gestapo commands, camp regime, words that flail at cowering heads. *Raus! Aufstehen!* Words sharp and precise, slicing off the mother tongues of millions. *Judensau. Scheissjude.* Taunts that rout and exult and wallow in filth.

*

Twilight hour on the lanai. Pain has abated for the moment. She sits leaning forward, good hand clenched around the trembler, peering at the orange streak of sky above some Australian pines. A string of pelicans sweeps down low over the lake, wheels above our heads, then up and away. Her face softens in the evening light, sheds decades. My young and hearty mother sits by me again. Beyond our line of vision the Florida sun plunges into the sea. Shadows deepen. Orange fades to black. Night swallows day. TV screens and floodlights take over.

*

She comes to me in the middle of the night. I feel her breath on my face and the bed heave as her dead weight drops beside me.

"I can't sleep," she sobs. "The pain."

I leap up and away.

"I'll get you the Tylenol. I think you can have another one now." The digital clock on the bedside table says it's three twenty-three.

"No," she moans. "It makes me sick to my stomach."

"I'll call the hospital."

"Just let me lie here beside you for awhile." She tucks her feet under the rumpled sheet. Her face blends with the shadows, her body looms large and clammy with sweat under her brushed-nylon nightgown.

"You go back to sleep," she whispers. "I'll be very still."

I switch on the table lamp and she stares up at me with tormented, pleading eyes. She shuts them again, as if guessing how they jeopardize her chances.

"Mama, maybe I really should..."

"All I want is to lie here. Is that so much for a mother to ask?"

I switch off the light and lie down on my back beside her, stiff, hands folded on my stomach, holding myself as separate as possible and yet feeling the invasion of her sweat, smell, restlessness, desire for me to stroke her hair as of old when I was a little girl and she begged in laughing tones "Do *krabbele, krabbele* in my hair" and I played with her stiff thick locks imagining my fingers marching through a forest.

She looms all around me, a devouring dragon. (*There once was a witch who turned into an owl at night and swooped down on maidens lost in the forest...*)

I lie still pretending to sleep and so does she, it seems, until I hear a rumble beside me, sound of a plough pushing gravel, her dragon-snore. I pull the sheet up around her, slip out of the room and to the living-room couch, which is safe and narrow and admits only one.

*

She used to come into my room after the lights were out when I was much too old to be checked on or tucked in. The obscene creak of floorboards announced her coming, her hand on the doorknob, so careful yet relentless, turning, opening. She burst in on my cave-world, my dreams of mouths and kisses, my body rocking, my hand probing. I lay still. I wished I could lie stiller. I wished myself dead. She crept in, knelt down, her eyes boring into the dark with her love and lonliness and fears for me.

"*Mein Kind*, my treasure," she breathed into the blankets, while I made my chest rise and fall in a steady, untouchable, clock-ticking rhythm.

Something looms above my head. Her hand moves closer, tentative, touches the outer layer of my hair, strokes. She strokes the air around me, so careful and so crushing. She wants to wrap me up tight in motherlove. Get out, get out, get out. The words hurl themselves against my skull. Words that would slash open the darkness, cut into her heart.

*

Codeine sleep, finally. Heavy, obliterating. She doesn't groan. She doesn't dream. I lie rigid and awake, aware of alien sounds. Hum and gurgle of air conditioners, buzz of spotlights and invisible security devices. Golden Gate's protective army.

Snatches of song bounce round in my mind. A word, half a word, riding the back of a half remembered tune. How does it go? I meant to ask earlier but in the scramble of the day, the meals, medications, manoeuvring, I forgot. *Wieder, Flieder,...*tra, la, la. Next door she snores. The rough noise of overused plumbing.

Snatches of stories, chopped off tales. How does it go? Mother Holle spread her snow all over the world. Snow like feathers in every crack and crevice, smoothing out the jagged edges, the jutting stone, tucking in the sleeping earth. I want to go back to her, to my room, kneel beside the bed and sing her a lullabye. Sing to the air above her head. A song that guards but doesn't wake. An old song that imitates the sigh of pines. "*Leise, leise,...*shhhh."

Who will share my country when you're gone?

Who will speak my language?

The Field

BY SANDRA NICHOLLS

My mother got up every morning as if she had erased the day before. I guess that's what my father had found so attractive about her. There were no consequences to anything. He came from a family where grudges were held for a long time, nursed and then allowed to fester. Once my dad's brother had made a wisecrack to me about why my father never seemed to have enough money to buy a new car, and after I told my father we didn't see Uncle Arthur for years. With my mother she could strip away the things she didn't want to remember like sheets off a bed.

Although we ended up on the East Coast, my mother and father met and married in Montreal, when, as my mother said, it was a city filled with romance. My mother was working in a gallery then, and my father came in to buy a painting. The way I imagined them then was like a painting too — full of light and possibilities. I'd seen photographs — a handsome couple, my Uncle Arthur had remarked, and I agreed with him, running my fingers over their posed and smiling faces. I could almost touch the luster of my father's black hair, the fuzzy warmth of his sweater. My mother's waist was so small then my father could just about wrap his hands around it.

It was 1982 when they moved to Ottawa, the year I was born. I think they pictured me skating on the canal and swimming in the Gatineau lakes in the summer. My father was a mathematician, but there wasn't a lot of steady work once the government departments that hired him began to cut back their budgets. My father had to find another way to make a living, and he ended up teaching high school math in a crummy little town called Prospero. We moved there the summer I turned 15, and I hated it from the moment we arrived.

Only 4000 people lived in Prospero. It actually had a main street called Main Street, and parking meters that cost a dime. Out on the highway the "Right to Life" sign that welcomed you into Prospero had a giant plastic blue rose on it, and I came to hate that rose, all it stood for in terms of smug little-townness, all the fakery of its welcome. My mother had to leave her friends, her job as an editor for a small decorating magazine, with her own office and stationery that had her name on it. What I hated was leaving my old room, knowing my way around, everything I thought I knew.

Prospero sounded romantic, from a distance. If you traveled in the car for twenty minutes in almost any direction you'd come to the sea. The land stuck out like a thumb into the Atlantic, and there were beaches down most of the unmarked gravel roads that snaked off the through-road. I seldom saw anyone on those beaches, because even in the summer the water was so cold you didn't even want to poke your toe in it. The best part of the beach was a whole shoreline of sedimentary rock that was gradually falling apart. You could just pick off a sheet of rock with your hands and break off the layers until you found a fossil. My favourite was all pockmarked with the impressions of shells, but before I could get it home it just disintegrated in my hands, and it made me feel kind of queasy to think all that rock was just breaking down in front of us.

Prospero's big claim to fame was the local hospital, St. Martha's, which was the biggest for miles around and had a fancy new birth wing with armchairs and pink lighting. Most of the people who struggled there to have their babies lived in even smaller towns around Prospero, or on farms, and they'd never seen luxury like St Martha's.

"What kind of hospital was I born in again?" For some reason I asked this question a lot.

"It was like Dracula's castle," my mother replied, referring to the birth wing of the Royal Victoria Hospital. "Way up high on the mountain, all grey and foreboding. Ghastly, really."

"Wasn't that where they did the CIA experiments?" I knew the answer, but I asked anyway.

"I think so. Yes." My mother's memory would then start to go murky.

"Did you scream when I was born? Was it awful?"

"No, no, dear, nothing like that. At least that I can remember. We were just happy to have this healthy baby." My mother had a plate of raw diced chicken in her hands, ready to fry in the wok. "We were just happy."

"Aren't you supposed to remember this stuff? It's pretty important, right?" My mother dropped the chicken into the wok and the steam shot up with a sizzle and obliterated her face in a cloud of white.

"What's important is that you're here, sweetie, that's the main thing." But I was preoccupied with the CIA, all that forgetting, the grey towers of the hospital. I suspected my mother whitewashed the whole thing, and it made me feel invisible, as if part of me had been sealed over.

Our house in Prospero faced out over an open field, but there was nothing to look at. When we lived in the city we used to take drives to the country and we'd admire the fields as we went by, fields deep purple with loosestrife or dotted with cows. But this field just sat there, lumpy and overgrown. People dumped whatever they didn't want on it, although they did their best to hide it in the long grass. Old high chairs, broken lamps, tires, rolls of chicken wire, whatever. Over time things rusted and cracked, took on new shapes. A well-beaten path led through the field to the back of Pearson's Variety, but my mother and I never took the path. We stayed on the road and went the long way when we wanted something. "You're to stay out of that field," my mother told me, "you never know what might be there." "Or who," we both piped up in unison, and laughed. We laughed, but I think my mother took that field as a kind of personal affront.

Behind our house was our yard, and compared to our city lot it was like a football field. It was one of the selling points my father used when he was trying to convince my mother to go to Prospero. All that room for a garden, he'd said. My mother was an avid gardener back in

Ottawa, and every year she'd order the seed catalogues and set up the little egg cartons with peat moss on shelves in the kitchen and little things would sprout, a process I always found truly incredible. Trying to garden in Prospero was another matter altogether, because the soil had so much clay in it. We had to order a shovel from the Sears catalogue store, the only source of most things in Prospero, and when we went down to pick it up it was a horrible bright purple colour, but we took it anyway, because otherwise it was another three weeks on order. We bought peat moss and sheep shit and together my mother and I attempted to dig a flower bed. I didn't really like gardening — the dirt and the worms and everything, but I didn't think she should have to tackle it all alone. The first time my mother tried to dig it up her boots got stuck in the clay and dad and I had to pluck her out of them like a rabbit from a hat. The boots never did get pulled out of the ground — we just laid the peat moss and the top soil right over them, as if they weren't there. She tried to plant the little seedlings, but Prospero was always windy, and they'd just sort of bend over in the wind, and then when it rained they just got plastered into the mud.

Some people would say that my mother tried to make the best of it, and she couldn't be criticized for that. But I didn't want her to. I wanted her to admit that she hated Prospero as much as I did. How could she not hate it? You couldn't even go to the movies — there was only one theatre in town and the owner had a liking for movies like *Rambo* and *Lethal Weapon*, which played for weeks on end. The winters were long and tough. Bingo and church suppers seemed like the local excitement. But she wouldn't say anything bad about it. The more she tried to defend Prospero, the more she betrayed me. She and Joey Sinclair.

Joey Sinclair was our next door neighbour. I'll never forget the first time I saw him. One arm was bent, nestled close to his body, as if he was cradling a bird or trying to keep something from falling out of his jacket pocket. The other arm acted like a ski pole, hauling him forward. One leg didn't seem to want to bend at all. As he got closer I could see his face, the teeth broken and yellowed, and his hair matted and greasy and sticking out in clumps. As he came up the steps I heard

32

the sound I would come to know so well — a bang followed by a kind of scraping as one leg was brought up to meet the other. He was wearing old army fatigues and cowboy boots. As he began to pound on the door, I imagined I could smell him too, a pungent mix of dirt and neglect. Joey and his two brothers lived right next door, along with their parents, in a house that was smaller even than ours.

I was staring out the front window, across to the field, waiting for my mother to turn the stereo on so we could practice dancing. Despite where we were, my mother was determined that I should learn all the social graces, and dancing was one of them. We liked to dance to the old crooners like Johnny Mathis or Frank Sinatra, or our favourite, Nat King Cole. I'd just heard the needle drop on to the old vinyl record, that pinprick of sudden static, when I caught sight of Joey lumbering along the path through the field towards our house.

"You're not going to answer the door, are you?" I moved back a little from the window, and pulled the curtains around my face. "Are you?"

Looking at my mother through the sheers I knew what the answer would be. Nat crooned from the stereo, with his terrible French accent: "Darling, je vous aim beaucoup, je ne say pas what to do."

"We can't just pretend we're not at home." My mother's hand went up to her hair, straightening it out as if she were in front of a mirror. "I'm sure he's harmless."

My mother went to the door and opened it. We were both wearing long black velvet skirts, our dancing clothes, and it must have seemed a little odd, in the middle of the afternoon. I noticed that some of the dust from the curtains had brushed against my skirt and I moved away from the window. You could see the dust motes hanging in the air where a cone of light opened in from the door. It was like being woken from a trance, or a deep dreamy sleep, and it made me cross and irritable. I glared over at the stranger. Joey tucked his bad hand inside the pocket of his navy windbreaker and introduced himself.

"Hey, how's it goin, eh? The name's Joey. I live right next door."

My mother, ever polite, extended her hand, before she realized that one of his hands was useless. She tried to retract it, but it was too late, and Joey had already put out his other hand, and so they had this awkward backwards handshake, and then my mother introduced herself.

"Oh, I know, I know. The old man's down at the school, right?"

I saw her hand go up to her hair again, although it was perfect. She wouldn't let on anything was bothering her. Joey peered around the doorframe and grinned at me, yellow teeth and all. I scowled. He must have been about 25 but he was like a child. Meanwhile the strings played like velvet in the background although everything had been ruined as far as I was concerned.

"That's Samantha. My daughter."

I just stood there in the living-room. Joey was still on the door-step, trying to see past me into the house. I wanted to close the door, send him away, get back to our dancing. With my face close beside my mother's, and the warm sweet smell of her hair, I could imagine I was dancing with my one true love, someone I truly believed would come. And here was our idiot neighbour. To me, Joey wasn't just our neighbour, he was the town, the whole, stupid, boring town. And there they were, him and my mother, having a conversation. Well, it wasn't really what you could call a conversation. Joey talked in monologues, and he didn't need you to talk back to him.

"Oh, Prospero? It's wild out there, eh? Better believe it. Wild and crazy."

Joey was convinced. Prospero was a town seething with excitement and intrigue. Somehow I'd just failed to see it.

"I'm gettin out of here though. Gettin out next week." He scratched his head and examined his fingernails, squinting in the shadow of our front porch. "Gonna take the bike and head for Toronto." He shook his head. "Yep. Nothin going on here."

Everything and nothing, it was all the same. Joey's world went no further than Pearson's Variety. His yard was littered with old machines which were supposed to take him out of Prospero and on to excitement, the idea that seemed to harness all the energy of his being. He told my father he could fix anything, and although I watched from my bedroom window the damaged machinery pile up in his back yard, I knew that wasn't true either. I knew exactly what it took to really repair something, and Joey just didn't have it. "Yep," he'd say, hunched over a rusted out motorcycle, "gonna fix up this baby. Get outta here."

But the weeks came and went, and Joey was still there. And so were we. I came to despise the way my mother stood there at the door, always patient, never actually letting him in, but never actually telling him to leave either. Even the tilt of her head began to irritate me, the way she let him blather on.

"He's out of touch," my mother would say, dreamily, staring out over the field, "out of touch."

The summer days in Prospero were long and listless and my mother tried to think of things to do. My father was busy, so mostly we went to the beach by ourselves. He was kind of an inventor, as well as being good with numbers. He was always peering into the back end of a piece of machinery, trying to figure out how it worked. Unlike Joey, he could fix things, at least if he put his mind to it. His favourite spot was his workshop, which was all instruments and tubes, prongs, oscillators, black boxes that glowed and beeped, timers, calibrators, measuring devices, things with dials that were sensitive to even the slightest pressure. Shelves ran to the ceiling and instrument cases and microscopes were toppled in piles and covered in dust. Some of the machinery was broken, but my father kept everything, convinced that one part might come in handy for another machine. Most of our household gadgets contained transplants from other gadgets, small circuit boards, tubes and levers like hearts and bundles of wired tissue.

There were dozens of those miniature plastic drawer cabinets, filled with circuits, bits of wire, screws, rivets, and tiny parts, although the one he was looking for was always the one that had dropped on the floor. Sometimes he pressed me into service with a flashlight and a magnifier. "Now, the thing you're looking for is no bigger than the head of a pin," he'd say, and I'd groan. Once I tried to pick up what I thought was a sparkling piece of tiny but vital machinery with the flat nub of my finger, but it turned out to be a sharp glass fragment and it drove straight up through my finger and left blood all over the carpet.

I didn't understand anything my father worked on, and neither did my mother, and he never let us forget it. He made himself a pair of what I called X-ray glasses, but they were really just magnifying lenses attached to a black plastic strap that went round his head. The lenses were at the ends of small cylinders which stuck out over his eyes like insect antennae, and they enabled him to work with both hands and still see what he was doing. "Look," he'd say, "see this," and he'd point to some tiny mechanism with a pair of tweezers. Since I didn't have the advantage of the "X-ray glasses," which made him look like something out of a bad 1950's film about atomic mutation, I had to bend and squint to see. Once I bumped right into the protruding lenses and when I looked up and into them my father's eyes were enormous and liquid, the eyes of a creature I didn't recognize. But he surprised me one morning by producing a duplicate pair out of his pocket at breakfast, my own customized set, and even my mother had to laugh at the sight of us, hunched over his desk, like two crazed insects inspecting our prey. We all had a good laugh over that, and for a while I had a glimpse of what my father saw, the orderly and precise world of tiny objects made big, the design revealed and made clear.

"Well, we're off." My mother would shout from the doorway, her hands full of picnic stuff, sandwiches and a thermos of coffee, towels, sunbloc, magazines, sunglasses, "See you later."
But my father was usually down in his workshop, or in the living-room, listening to music, oblivious, headphones on. The faint, spindly strands of symphonies leaked into the air from somewhere far away. Some mornings I'd shout out awful things to him. "So long,

fathead." "Why don't you drop dead." And one morning, when my mother was out of earshot, "Fuck you." I hesitated for a while at the door. I wasn't sure if I he'd heard me or not. But anyway, he never said anything, and mum would close the door behind us, and we'd leave. I think she heard me though, because as we drove out to the highway, past the plastic rose and the trailer park, she'd have this unpleasant little smile on her face.

That was the summer I just hung out with my mother. It was easier that way. A few mornings I'd bring up the idea at breakfast of going to the community centre to join something, or knocking on a few doors where I'd seen some kids my age, but my mother looked so crest-fallen I just couldn't do it. "You mean you're not going to come with me today to the beach?" "Yes, Samantha," my father would say, disap-pearing out of the room, "go and keep your mother company. There'll be lots of time for friends once school starts." I liked her company fine, and I felt sorry for her at first. My father was so busy preparing for school, and after all, she'd been dragged here too. I felt like we were one of those families in a Jane Austen book, suddenly forced to come down in the world through circumstances which weren't our fault. Summer turned to fall while we sat at the beach, and September seemed to happen suddenly, at least to us, the wind grown bitter overnight, and the rocks we collected painfully cold in our hands.

September meant that two of us would be leaving the house every morning and leaving my mother alone. My mother prepared for it by wearing herself out with activity: pressing my father's clothes, pol-ishing his shoes, buying me stuff for school. She tried at first, of course, to do the things she thought full-time mothers should do. She baked muffins, washed floors, swept the porch even as the first flakes of snow began to fall. Sometimes she'd be there when I got home, leaning with her chin propped at the top of the broom handle, gazing blankly at the field, and I wondered how long she'd been standing there. School didn't turn out to be as bad as I had thought. We all hated Prospero, and we all wanted to be somewhere else, even the kids who were born there. We figured Prospero was great if you were three, or ten, but not for a teenager. There just wasn't anything to do. But at least we could do nothing together, that is, if my mother let me out.

Dad spent most evenings preparing classes, marking papers and falling asleep over his desk. One night he got so mad at a student's math paper he tore it up and threw it across the room. "Idiots," he shouted, and I remembered that he used to work on big projects for the government, reading through papers that came in envelopes marked "Top Secret," and that I used to find it funny how he sneaked around with them, as if either my mother or I could understand them anyway. So my mother and I watched movies we rented from Pearson's, and I did my homework propped up beside her on the couch. I used to have trouble with math, and my mother was no help, but I couldn't bear to ask my father. "It's so simple," he'd say, and my mind would go blank. My friends would ask me over, or to hang out somewhere, but I couldn't deal with my mother's disappointment if I made other plans. "But I already rented this movie, sweetie. Didn't you want to see this one?"

I started to resent my father's absence, the way he made himself a martyr. I heard them arguing one night after I went to bed.

"I didn't want to come here. You did." There was a touch of hysteria in my mother's voice, a touch of something crazed.

"You think I like teaching these little idiots? You think that's what I studied for seven years for? To do this?" I heard something drop, a book or something hard and flat.

There was a weird creepy little laugh that snorted out of my mother's throat. "Oh yes, well we all know you're much more intelligent than the rest of us, don't we." And then I heard her walk out of the room and into the kitchen. Then the door to my father's workshop slammed. I started to wonder why he had ever married my mother in the first place. And why he'd had me. We must have both been disappointments.

It was around that time that Joey started coming to the door at all hours, day and night, even once the snow had come and stayed. He never got past the bristly welcome mat; he just stood in the doorway, as if there was an invisible wall there. I got used to the pounding, but I still hated the way my mother went to the door every time, shivering and listening to Joey rattle on about nothing while the snow formed little white pyramids at his feet. My father ignored him. I couldn't stand him. And I didn't like the way my mother could say no to me but not to my father, and not to Joey.

The word at school was that Joey had been hit by a truck when he was only a kid, but in that small town we always wondered if it wasn't some sort of birth defect that kept Joey the way he was. But Joey had bought into the story too, and he turned it into a personal victory.

"Oh yeah, they took me to the hospital, but I wasn't going to stay in no hospital."

"Why not?" my mother asked, leaning against the wooden door frame, muffin batter dripping off her spoon and on to the floor.

"Don't trust no doctors. I was outta there right quick."

My mother hates doctors too, and tries to stay away from them, but with Joey she simply grunted and nodded, letting Joey carry on, his flow punctuated now and then by the question that soon became a running family joke: "What's goin on, eh?" The silent answer that hung around my mother like a cloud of smoke was always the same: nothing, nothing at all.

Somehow it never occurred to my mother to leave my father. Or if it did, she didn't tell me. She made the dinners and made the beds, asked my father politely about his days at the school, kissed him quickly on the cheek. My father didn't seem to care, as long as I was there. But once in a while my mother would explode. That's the way I used to see it. All my father had to do was criticize her for something she'd forgotten to do around the house, or for picking up the wrong sort of cheese at the Sobeys, and she'd start throwing things and screaming. It terrified me, and my father wouldn't go near her. I guess it was something like a fit, all those sheets winding tighter and tighter until she was choking on her own anger.

The next day it would all be forgotten. "Good morning, sweetie," she'd say from the kitchen, "want some pancakes?" Dad would wink at me as he left for school, his lunch tucked under his arm, and I'd sit at the breakfast table, trying to figure out why I'd lost my appetite, my hands digging in my pockets for somewhere to put themselves, the

scene around me like a Norman Rockwell calendar. Soon I'd go kind
of numb, and start smiling too, and I'd leave for school wondering if all
families acted this way. Why couldn't she tell me what was wrong? I
put my arms around her once, the morning after she'd ripped a picture
off the wall and smashed it in frustration; I wanted her to cry, to break
down, tell me something, but she was like stone, and she kept her arms
stiff at her sides, a kind of human wall, and she wouldn't cry, not even
for me. I wanted to hate her, but I couldn't even do that.

She went to a doctor in Prospero once, and I went with her
although she made me stay in the waiting room. I've often wondered
what she told him, because when she came out we went to the phar-
macy and got a prescription for some pills which she told me were for
headaches. But she'd never mentioned headaches to me, and that night
I heard her talking on the phone to one of her friends from Ottawa,
something she rarely ever did. "Little pink pills," she'd said, "I can't
believe it. I've turned into one of those awful housewife clichés." I
don't think she ever took them, because the prescription bottle stayed
hidden in a corner of the kitchen cupboard for months, and the name
of the little pills grew fainter and fainter with time.

I saw my parents as living separate lives. I couldn't figure out
why they just didn't make it official. The thought that they might be
doing it for my sake was more than I wanted to admit. Separately I got
on with them great, but together they seemed to suck all the joy out of
each other, like milk out of a bottle. They were civil, of course, but there
were huge gaps.
    "Let's go out for dinner tonight, what do you say?" My father on
a Friday night, all flushed with his paycheque.
    "Okay dear, where do you want to go?'
    This was kind of a joke, since Prospero only had three restau-
rants, and one of them was a pizza parlour.
    "You choose the spot!"
    "I really don't care. Wherever you want."
    " How about Lucy's?"
    "I'm not really dressed for Lucy's, but if *you* want to go there..."
    "Oh fuck, never mind."

My father didn't suggest doing anything together very often, and I guess it always took us by surprise. We had to be ready when he did, we had to spring into action whenever he decided he needed us as a family. But we weren't. We'd made it more comfortable to stay in, as if going out would make it too obvious that something was wrong. A whole meal had passed in near silence once, at the diner, the three of us pasted to the orange fake leather booth. Another time, although each of them spoke to me, neither of them spoke to each other, and I felt like a badminton birdie, being batted back and forth between them.

One night at dinner my mother announced that she had found a part-time job. Her face was all pink with excitement as she slapped big piles of mashed potatoes on to our plates.

"It's only filing, but it's at a lawyer's office, right down on Main Street. Three afternoons a week, so I won't be able to cook those nights." My mother poured some gravy on to Dad's potatoes and it sloshed down the side and began dripping off the edge of the table on to his pants. "For Christ sake," Dad shouted, scraping his chair back and wincing as the hot gravy burned through his pant leg. I could almost feel her words going backwards down her throat, the air go silent. Sometimes I thought their problems were just a matter of bad timing.

It was kind of a sick joke that my father chose that time to set up intercoms that he'd built all over the house, so we could talk to each other from any room. I think my mother suspected it was so he could stay in his workshop longer and not have to come out, although she never said. We had to wander all over the house testing them out, although the speakers were always too loud and you couldn't make out anything. I'd be sitting in the kitchen with my mother and this scratching blast of sound would suddenly shoot out of the speaker and send you to the ceiling. Finally my father disconnected them, although the little black boxes stayed up on the walls, looking like they belonged there, but dead as doornails.

We even had an intercom at the front door, and I imagine the people who lived next door on either side thought we were spies. My mother never got to know the neighbours. Of course, it didn't seem to occur to them either. The fact that my dad was a teacher seemed to brand us as big shots, and of course, we were from the city, from away. Joey's family never wanted to look us in the eye, for some reason, and his mother didn't really seem like my mother's type. She was a little fat woman who wore the same thing all the time, whatever the weather: a brown suede bomber jacket that looked as if it had been left out all night in the rain, a flowered skirt with giant pink poppies on a black background, and wellington boots, rain or snow or freezing drizzle. She had a sour, puzzled expression on her face most of the time, and she just didn't look like she'd be fun to have in for coffee. That's how my mother put it.

Then there was Irene, the lawyer's secretary, who lived right down the street. I used to wait for my mother sometimes, after school, in the office. I watched her feeding piles of beige folders into dark green filing cabinets, and the lawyer come and go, muttering to himself and puffing at a cigarette, his shirt hanging out, his fingers yellow and pudgy as sausages. Irene never said much while I was there, just answered the phone and watched, slack-jawed, as my mother worked. It was as if the word "outsider" was branded across my mother's forehead, but I didn't really know whose fault it was.

My mother got her notice after a few weeks. They'd decided to finish the filing themselves, the letter said, what with financial considerations and all. "What a bunch of jerks," I said, "Don't they know a good thing when they see it?" My mother held the yellow-stained letter in her hands and said nothing, folded it neatly and put it away in the kitchen drawer, next to the coupons and the brown paper lunch bags. That was the same day she came to pick me up from school and miraculously her handbag was still perched on the roof of the car where she'd left it. I watched our old blue Pontiac round the corner and pull up in front of the school where I was hanging out with some friends.

"Hey Sammy, what's that on top of your mother's car?" Beth-Ann was pointing at the car and snickering, and my mother was leaning over the passenger seat and peering through the glass of the window, thinking we were all having a jolly good time. I was so embarrassed I could have died. "What's the matter, is your mother some kind of idiot?" I heard someone whisper.

The word slashed me like a knife. I grabbed the purse from the roof of the car and got in the car as fast as I could. My friends were all laughing.

"Come on, let's go." I said testily, staring straight ahead. "Let's *go.*"

"What are you doing with my purse?" My mother's face was genuinely surprised.

"You left it on the top of the car." My voice was dry and sarcastic. "Come on, let's get out of here."

My mother shifted suddenly into gear and we lurched away from the school. She was wearing sunglasses, and little tears began trickling down from underneath them, although she said nothing, and neither did I.

My mother tried to talk to my father about her disappointment. "You'll find something better," he'd said, and that was that. He looked over at her, across the table and the bowls of food, as if to say: is there anything else? He'd started opening up his mail, already moving on. "Sure, I'm sure I will." she'd said, to herself, or to me, or to the placemat. It didn't really matter. She got up and filled the coffee machine, but she'd already filled it and the water poured all over the counter and down to the floor and I don't think she noticed until her socks were totally soaked. My father had already left the room, and was heading downstairs to his workshop.

It wasn't until I came home to find that she'd packed away all our old forty-five records into a box and dumped them in the trash that I realized the mother I thought I knew was slipping away from me, the way bubbles disappear when you're lying in the bathtub. You barely notice, and quietly they disappear. I guess I should have said something, but I didn't.

It was just our luck to be living in Prospero when we got hit by the worst Maritime storm in twenty-five years. Snow whipped up against the windows and the doors and pelted like giant rocks against the plastic siding. The wind trapped between the siding and the walls made the house moan and shingles snapped off the roof and crashed to the ground. It was so cold that when I tried opening the back door it was like opening one of those heavy metal doors to a deep freeze — tons of cold steam poured into the house — you could imagine carcasses hanging from hooks out there. From the windows the hills were invisible — it was just snow and blackness. My mother and I prowled around the house like a couple of cats trapped in a barn. Soon we could hardly see out the windows at all, except for the vague haloes of the headlights on my father's car as he pushed up the driveway.

We'd all read about the storms and we knew the damage they could do. My mother checked in the freezer to see how much food was left in there, and the cans and the jars of rice and pasta in the basement. We didn't say much to each other, though we were somehow thrust together by the force of the storm outside. My father banged around for a while in his workshop, as if he could find something in there that would help. The town and everybody in it seemed far off, nestled away in their own houses. It seems funny now, but I wondered how long I was going to be stuck inside.

The beeping of the microwave announced that the big pot of lamb stew my mother'd defrosted was ready to eat. She shouted to my father in the basement and brought the plates to the table. I was kind of enjoying the storm, from the inside looking out, the way it brought us together and made our enemy so easy to identify. We could all talk about the storm. Somehow if we couldn't see out the windows we could forget where we were. I was about to spear a forkful of lamb when the pounding at the door made us all jump.

As usual, my mother got up to answer it, like an idiot. I dropped my fork down on the plate and it clattered off the side and spattered the table with grease. Joey stood there, ankle-deep in snow, no hat and the wind wailing around his head. He just stood there, staring in at us, our plates heaped with steaming food. Not even the worst storm in twenty-five years could keep Joey out of our lives. My mother's head tilted a bit to one side as cold steam shot in around my feet and I began to shiver. My father was staring into his plate, waiting for something to happen. I couldn't stand it any longer. I got up and went to the door

44

and told him to come in, and then I shut it behind him, leaving my mother staring into a closed door. It shut with a kind of swoop, as the frigid air and the snow were sealed outside, and after the howling of the storm the room seemed unnaturally quiet.

I brushed past my mother and went back to the table. "It's fucking freezing out there," I asserted, to the plate. My mother just stood there, with her back to us. Maybe a minute passed, and then she turned and came back to the table, her eyes looking everywhere but at me. We all watched and waited for Joey to say something. My mother pushed her food around on her plate, but when dad lifted his fork to his lips, she threw him a look that made him drop it like a hot brick.

Joey stood in a pool of melting snow, grinning all over his face and looking around. I hated him just then.

"Some night out there, eh?" I rolled my eyes back at this small town understatement.

No one answered him. The back of my throat felt raw and constricted and the room was still cold from the door being left open so long. I felt so trapped I could hardly breathe. Finally my father said something.

"You know Joey, I can't imagine anybody being stupid enough to go out in this weather." My father, ever the logician.

Joey was still grinning. I noticed his bad hand hanging down from beneath his windbreaker, like some dead thing.

My mother went next.

"You should be wearing a hat, Joey. Why aren't you wearing a hat?" She got up and went to the wooden seat by the door. It opened like a chest and we kept our hats and mitts and ear muffs and scarves in it. She started rummaging around, muttering to herself about this hat being too small, or too big, or the wrong shape. The hats and scarves were flying across the room as she tossed them over her shoulder. "Wrong colour."

Then Joey spoke up, with a kind of lunatic sanity. "I don't need no hat."

Like an automaton, my mother got up and walked back to the table.

"The snow was so bad, eh? Couldn't see a goddamn thing." Joey got suddenly animated and tried to gesture with both his arms. He looked like the straw man from the *Wizard of Oz*. "Snow's so wicked out there you couldn't see anything. My brother and his kid, eh? Out on the highway. I saw them. I saw them dead and all."

Joey kept telling us about how he'd got past the police, and how he'd seen his brother first. He was jabbering, but I guess we'd stopped listening.

My mother hadn't looked at me since I let him in, as if I was the one who brought in the bad news, as if it was my fault. I looked at her expression and it was blank, blank as a stone. She didn't even know which brother, which kid. I sat in silence in front of my plate, my jaw clenched and tense.

"Are you sure you wouldn't like a hat, Bobby?" I couldn't believe my ears. "I'm sure Sammy has one she could loan you." But Joey wasn't listening anyway and he just carried on. My father had said nothing.

"My own brother, eh? It's wild out there. Shouldn't been out there. Gonna have to be a funeral, but I ain't goin. I hate funerals."

He started to laugh, and wiped a hand over his eyes. "Hate doctors and funerals."

"So do I," I heard my mother say, and then she started to laugh too, a wheezy sucked in sort of laugh. "Hate them with a passion." My father and I just stared holes into our plates. The sound of her laughing was making me sick.

Finally Joey said he had to go. My father mumbled something about letting us know if there was anything we could do, and my mother let him out, stepped straight through the puddles of melted snow in her sock feet, and right back through them again on her way to the table. We sat before our plates of cold stew in silence. Then they started talking. Just like that, as if nothing had happened.

"I can heat this up in the microwave, if you want."

My mother was talking to my father. Two people were dead. My voice was frozen in my throat.

"Just take a second."

My father handed over his plate, and my mother squelched over to the counter where the microwave was.

"I can't believe anyone would go out on a night like tonight." My father was scratching his chin and trying to look thoughtful.

"Neither can I. That poor family." The light from the microwave was pouring out into the kitchen, like something alien, and the plate of stew was spinning around and around inside, and I could see it through the little window. Even though I knew it was coming the sound of the beep made me jump. "Here you are."

A plate of steam passed in front of me. I swallowed a cold, half-chewed piece of carrot and then spit it out again. This was how it happened, this was how the forgetting started.

"What's the matter with you?" I was startled at the sound of my own voice as it broke through the kitchen like an arrow. "What the fuck is the matter with you?"

I don't really know what happened next. I remember the plate smashing and the stew splashing up on my leg, like cold paste. I saw my parents' mouths opening and closing but the words were like gibberish. I saw the door. Nothing else mattered. There was no storm, no fear, no sense. I don't know if anyone tried to stop me. I don't know if it took five seconds or five minutes. I just ran blind, out into the night, and across the road to the field. I ran and ran until my feet got snagged in some chicken wire, and I fell face first into the snow.

I wondered for a moment if they'd stop to put on their jackets and boots. I'm sure they would have, once they'd realized that I was actually gone. I wondered who would come, my mother or my father, or both of them. I managed to crane my neck around, and when I looked up at the sky it was like staring into the dome of some great black cave that was alive with a thousand white moths. So beautiful. I tried tugging at my foot but it was useless. The more I tried to get away, the tighter the wires hooked around my ankle. I figured I'd forget everything if I could just get warm again. I heard the sound of my name being called, and I waited for someone to come.

Preserving Jars

BY SHARON HAWKINS

A Woman Is Drawing Her Mother

She sets out
five blue Staedtler pencils
sharpens each one to a point
touches them tentatively

soft ones to weave the shadows
harder ones for lines and seams
and edges
she is not an artist

she has erased her mother's face
ten times now
so it shines   illusory
like the face of a saint
in a holy picture

has worn the paper
thin as onion skin
in places
where the layers have lifted
around the eyes
about the mouth

she draws familiar strangers
a woman looking past her
another staring at the ground
she knits her mother's brow
she draws the back of her mother's head
she covers her mother's face
with aging hands

she draws a woman who is waiting
expectantly   for something
to happen
draws in convoluted lines
a young woman
who could have been her grandmother
and an old woman who   given time
might be herself

a woman draws her mother
slowly from memory's spool
threads her
painstakingly
through a small elusive eye.

Making Your Way Back

Where do mothers go when they leave you?
They close their eyes right there
in the kitchen, missing among the dishes,
buried up to their elbows in bread dough.
They get tied up in clothes lines
and missionary meetings, hide out
in the raspberry bushes, get lost
in the crosswords. It doesn't really matter where,
only, that they go, so quietly and so soon
and you don't know,
so you never think to memorize her eyes
her sound her smell the feel of her arms
around you, gone before you know them,
too soon to ever find your way back
if you ever have to, if you're ever
really hurt or really hungry.

You can look, and you will,
in other faces one day you will see her
sitting there in flowers, red ones mostly,
just at the edge of an endless forest.
She will speak to you and you will know her,
from some small place inside you will know
you have found her, you are limping
falling down, crawling, cradling your way back
through all the broken dishes, tangled cords
and bible stacks, past all the words
on all the pages, only words,
you are past that now, inarticulate,
you become your senses, all there is,
you wear your last garment, like the first,
made without pockets,
you burrow in, you think you want to stay, and slowly
you are healing, slowly filling up,
you make your way back to wherever
children go when they leave you.

Preserving Jars

Air from before the depression
is captured in the walls
of these jars:
streaking seed-like bubbles
caught in glass suspension
while they cooled
in the moulds
of the Dominion
Glass & Bottle Company.

And in this green Crown sealer,
flawed with the perfect
imprint of a single dragonfly wing
still trembling
from another century,
my grandmother packed blue
icicles, soaked twelve days in brine
with pickling spice and alum.

I have rescued them
from the root cellars of my mother
and my grandmothers,
disturbed the sanctuary
of million year old bugs
and spiders,
depending

on the season
I fill them now with cobalt
blue irises, ginger
snaps, cut geraniums,
or leave them
empty on the window sill
to collect reflections
and at times, the things I've taken
from my pockets.

And somewhere in the attic
there is one still filled
with the small serrated
edge photos I have of my mother
when she was young
and one
with the memory of a time
when I thought I could save her
by mixing all her Avon powder
with the perfume she wore on Sundays,
sealing it in a Mason jar
as though it were
a reliquary.

Geraniums

I can trace on my knees
the slow conquest of bicycles
and on my wrist the etching
of a bent nail, first
memory of my own blood
falling all around me, shaken
like bright, red petals
from my mother's best geranium.

When I held my own
hand in a towel and sat so still
in the doctor's leather chair
while he stitched and I counted
and recounted all the bottles
on the shelves, filled
with the same red medicine
he gave for every ache
and pain, I wondered
then, half wonder now,
if he made it
from geraniums.

Grandmother Dreams

Dreams of my grandmother wrapped
in her muskrat coat
where I bury my face down
to the soft fur beneath
the long shining outer hairs

in the back of the old Buick
at night, leaving home we are talking
about what we would do if we had forty
thousand dollars, we are talking
about all the possibilities

the wonder of having more
than we need in the country
where there is only the thin
blue needle in the circle
on the dashboard measuring
the speed of this retreat

and squares of yellow farmhouse
windows floating past us, the stars
like pinholes in a shadowbox
and the endless drifts gathering
like sheep behind snow fences

where I count her buttons in the dark
how they feel as smooth as amber,
touch the silk lining
at the end of her sleeve
where I slide my hand inside

there is only the hum
of wheels on dirt road
this warm soft light and the world
all white beyond the window

like milk in a bottle
in the morning, the bowls
she takes from the sideboard
are sapphire blue depression glass
curved
where I cup my hand to feel
the warmth of soft
boiled eggs and broken bread,
and she serves me
apple juice in her cranberry
thumb-print goblets with stems
and at night
she and I
sit at the kitchen table
last thing
before bed having toast
with sprinklings
of cinnamon and demerara sugar
just talking
just
for a moment I think
if she ever gives me
anything, I want
the sapphire bowl and the cranberry goblet,
I want
those amber buttons,
want to carry them
always
in my pocket.

Tomato Marmalade

I make my way to you
where the lawn has captured
a few more feet of your garden
measuring the progress of cataracts
edging across your eyes

but you have a harvest nonetheless
and I have come home for it

you want to give me marmalade
six jars
made fresh this morning
knowing I was coming and so
many tomatoes this year
it's what you have, you offer
a mother's love in glass
labelled and dated
sterile, tightly capped

so this is how you want to do it
with fruit and vegetables
holding out something to save
and preserve us
from leftovers of childhood pushed
to the back of the fridge, forgotten
and the seals breaking down
and the lids coming off
and the spoilage

when I ask to see the recipe
you pass it on as it was
handed down to you
the way you've always done it:
a dash of hot red pepper
soda, a pinch, to cut the acid
the measure of spice
to the size of your thumb
sugar and vinegar equal
and tomatoes, skinned
and quartered
and seeded

six jars are too much
three more than I can take
and I grow my own tomatoes

ripening now, forgiveness
hangs between us, green
too early yet for picking.

Eye Contact (1)

So you must wonder
how it is
that a woman can sit
with you
for six years
in the same room
only five feet away
without looking
and wonder what she does
when she closes her eyes
is she spinning a web
to join herself to you
does she imagine
a great sheltering tree
so full of leaves
that there must be
one unnoticed leaf
where she could fasten
strands so fine
so insubstantial
light as gauze
laid gently on a wound
does she imagine
she could suspend herself there
in gossamer sanctuary
waiting out the winter
you must so often wonder
will she fly, ever fly?

Eye Contact (2)

So you must wonder
how it is
that a woman can sit
for six years
in the same room
only five feet away
without looking
and wonder what she does
when she closes her eyes
is she spinning like a wheel
and has she noticed
the character of wheels
how hard it is
to see where they begin
with another woman
where they end
how they blur
when they're turning?

Eye Contact (3)

So you must wonder
how it is
that a woman can sit
with you
only five feet away
without looking
and wonder what she does
when she closes her eyes
for six years
is she spinning a thread
turned between finger and thumb
winding a spindle
a little more
at each round
of the wheel
gathering it unbroken
in the same room
you must wonder
will she weave it into cloth
will there be colours
will there ever be enough?

Eye Contact (4)

So you must wonder
how it is
that a woman can sit
with you
for six years
in the same room
and what she does
when she closes her eyes
is she spinning like a child
sometimes does with her arms
thrown out to the side
only five feet away
whirling like a top
inside her own vortex
is she testing
her equilibrium
you must wonder
without looking
when she leaves
does she ricochet
in the stairwell
does she weave her way
down the street?

Winter Solstice I

In the time of angels
and archangels
in the week of the winter solstice
the first real snow
the afternoon light
the days stretching already
and too soon toward summer

I walk for a time behind a woman
so much like my grandmother
the way she moves
her white hair
so much like her
that I expect she will turn
where I will turn
at the corner

where she pauses a moment
and I come so close
that I can see my reflection
in her glasses   a quiver
of longing   distinct
against the snow
in this different light

where she pulls her shawl
more closely around her
folds it
wings at her side
and continues on her way
while I follow

only with my eyes
by the light changing
red   then green

then red   then green
for as long as I can see
her white hair
how she looks   back
for a moment
long enough for me
to raise my hand
for her
to nod her head.

There are nine orders
in the hierarchy of angels
from cherubim and seraphim
worshipping and falling down
to angels and archangels
sometimes found
near the corner of First and Bank
when the winter light is so soft
there are no shadows
when even
in newly fallen snow
the footprints of a woman walking
disappear.

Something About Renewal

where can you find a stable and cows
at seven o'clock some morning
and a farmer who won't ask questions

won't think you mad
when you want to come in, want to sit
silent, watch the milking

breathe in the barn, the steamy fusion
of disinfectant, sharp ferment
and black earth sweetness

listen to the cows, their soft calling
to one another, breathing in time
the metronomic sluck sluck of milking machines

surely you can't tell him
you only want to think
quietly there, with those great familiar creatures

their sad eyes, baled heads, stretched udders, blue
veined, pressing for release, absorbed
in the giving, the milk thick, flowing warm

surely not tell him you want to close your eyes
and watch your mother disappear
for half a day each fall, into the dry corn

just before harvest, to walk the field alone
return after hours, saying something
about renewal, something about starting again

how can you tell him you only want to find
yourself there, visit for awhile
claim each pain, close your hand around it

only want to let the years weave themselves
into something whole and useful, wrap themselves
around you like a blanket of new skin.

Moving House

Mostly
it is because
there is more space,
and the rent is less,
and the heat is oil,
and I can walk to work from here
in twenty minutes.

I already know my neighbours
and they have an alpine garden
with edelweiss and thyme and veronica,
and everyone has a cat,
and someone said there are kestrels
in the summer
and I've never seen one.

And partly
because my preserving
jars will look good on the plate rail,
and there is morning sun
in the kitchen
where I can look out the window
and drink tea
with milk
from a glass
if I want.

And my plants will do well
in the sun porch,
and the curtains
just fit
in the living room.

And perhaps
because when I stood
the first time
in the space
between outside and inside,
the newel post
on the staircase
looked the same.

And I had the idea
that in the summer the moths would beat
against the window
on the verandah
like a heart out of rhythm.
And the trap door to the attic
would have the same rope
and pulley, the same
dark passage.

And probably the cedars
in the back yard
would have so many morning glories
twining in the branches
that a small child could hide there
easily enough.

And if the ground
were not frozen now,
I might dig beneath the pine tree
and find a white stone,
my mother's favourite broach.

And when an east wind blows
through the pine tree's branches,
it sounds like the wings of angels
hovering, trying
hard to hold their balance
falling sometimes
breaking
like a fever.

And I suppose
the ceilings are so high here
this house could echo silence,
or Vivaldi, the *Gloria in D major*
or Scarlatti, *Dixit Dominus*.

Gestures

She tells herself now
that she will live
alone forever, better
less complex
and yet sometimes
in the morning
and at five o'clock in the afternoon
and sometimes at around eleven
in the evening
she reaches out
her hand

or if there's time
to catch herself
she only lifts
a finger.

And Now The Garden

sighs in anticipation:
movement in the air,
clouds for the first time in ten days,
light fading
the last day of the week
of the summer solstice.

The tall plants
with no name by the fence, pulse
in wind from another place
another time, perhaps
some ancient cadence
danced by women gathering
under oaks at twilight.

This was another woman's garden.
Mine for only six unknowable months under snow
now slowly coming out
with such uncertain boundaries
such strange perennials.

She was a composter. I find
a peach pit sprouting and egg shells and strings
and this morning in the row
for the second planting of radishes,
a small piece of pink milk glass
curved slightly
from the kind of tea cup
that came free
in Puffed Wheat
in the Fifties.
And last month
in the first deep digging
there was an old hook rusted forever
into the eye
that once held someone's door closed.
I keep these things
for no good reason
except that they belong here.
Move them to a corner
where the hens and chicks
have settled between rocks and roots.
Add the small stones
I have brought with me
from wherever I have been.
and plant amongst them
two small pine tree sprouts
and three little cedars I found
growing in the lawn,
some sprigs of veronica
and at the back, grain amaranth
that will grow six feet tall in time
and will bend
and brood over them in storms
like a mother.

I Am Only Beside Her

I am beside the woman
in the bed. I am not her.
I am only beside her.
This is what I am thinking
how she has no breasts now
although once she did
I remember
and look for the first time
at her naked body, look
with the doctor young enough
to be my daughter
who asks me questions
for which I have no answers,
I should, I think
know it all, know
in detail all about the body
that gave me life,
and then my mother asks me
how my bicycle is working
do they sell lemon pie in the cafeteria
why do the bells ring so often
and why are there no windows here and is it day
or night and is it raining,
these things, I know,
I tell her everything,
read to her from the paper
spread across her stomach,
the leaves in the Agawa Canyon
how the people come from everywhere
the beauty
the walls rising red and green and yellow
stop, go wait, she is my mother
she is listening to the room
wants me to tell the woman in the next bed

not to drink milk if she takes iron
and I tell her, Mom
there are some things
that simply can't be said
and she nods
and she says
oh yes.

Private Alters

We had what was meant for us, divided,
few words, agreements made with eyes,
small gestures of the hand, a nod.
About the rest, we were decisive,
church bazaar, Salvation
Army, best friend, Food Bank, auctioneer...

There were things we should have thrown away.
We couldn't do it, we tried, really, all of us,
my aunts, my sister, me. We carried them
around the house, turned them in our hands,
set them down, picked them up. Piled them silently
on the livingroom floor, private
alters, stone upon stone that long afternoon

there were things that could go nowhere else
placed in boxes, carried home, set
in the downstairs hallway
already a narrow passage
where two people meet, only with difficulty.

Ten months, it has taken
that long to find places for the broken
handled rolling pin, the fifty-six mechanical pencils
the sheet music - her four versions
of *A Mighty Fortress*... paper bags
full of loose stamps: Edward
George, Victoria, Elizabeth as a young girl,
small bits of wool, the mitten pattern, slips
of rhyming poems from *Ladies Home Journal*
the spirit of my mother
her childhood scrapbook and the Robin Hood cookbook
every card she received when I was born, love
letter from my father, stones and shells
my mother's heart carried home. My mother's heart.

Red Becomes Red

BY NADINE MCINNIS

Quill. Even her name hurts me, a hook in my heart. Her name was a private joke. She broke the water inside me and I imagined her holding something sharp and wild in her hand, choosing the moment to be born. The three of us slept while the midwife sat in a chair beside us, watching for storm clouds forming. The angel passed over. Then I rose, left them there asleep, and when the moon lifted in the sky, went with her to the garden to plant the afterbirth. It had cooled slightly, a slippery spineless sea creature that swam away from me, leaping out of my hands before the hole was deep enough.

"Plant your tomatoes here. You'll have the sweetest crop," the midwife said.

"Red becomes red," I said, filled with such thankfulness. Stars swirled around above me. I was still a bit faint.

But now she's become like a squirming black dog clamped between my legs as I pull quills out with pliers before they work themselves into the brain. Quills can drive a dog mad.

A year has passed, and finally I can say her name, though still not to him. The door fans inwards, he brings a gust of air so cold I think it has frozen into this blinding light shattering onto the floor. I turn away just after I catch that look on his face. His eyes, watchful, bluer than they used to be, as though the water that drowned her is rising up inside him. I've seen him sweep it away with the back of his knuckle, looking down. A man's tears are always furtive as a running nose. Something to be dispensed with.

He steps out of his work boots and walks towards me with the empty ice-cream pail and places it on the counter where I'm sitting and smoking, still in my housecoat. I started smoking again, first time since adolescence, when the cold weather came. I wanted that desert burn in my throat

"The chickens have stopped laying again. Only one," he says. "Here, it's warm." And he reaches to place the egg still smeared with straw and shit in my hand.

The cold that swept in with him raises goose-bumps on my thigh where my legs are crossed at the knee. I shift away from him before the ugly thing is in my hand, lift the edge of the cloth and cover my leg. He turns away from me, keeping his face set in angry profile, a beard of stone, so that I'll know he's taken this personally. Mount Rushmore.

"Don't they have enough light?" I ask.

He dissolves and his attention rushes back towards me. A torrent of need.

"Not in this cold. And, Rachel, I mean cold. When's the last time you were outside?"

So, then it's my turn to leave my smoldering cigarette, a small light of comfort in the wilderness, and move to the window. The backyard blurs into the prairie behind, one undulating expanse of bleached snow. At this time in the morning, the light doesn't separate snow from sky, both go on forever, but it's better than being in town where the chimneys, comings and goings of cars and trucks, people breathing, leave everything enshrouded in a cloud of ice fog. During spells like this, you have to wear a scarf over your mouth to keep the ice crystals from scarring your lungs.

"Look's like a desert. Looks like sand."

"Don't," he says. He'll listen to no more, and he's gone, his truck throttling miserably to life as I watch through the window. He backs out without disconnecting the extension cord for the block heater. Bright orange pulls taut, then snaps. He'll have something else to keep him occupied when he comes back. Good for him.

Polydipsia — sustained excessive thirst, the kind of thirst that drives you to drink anything. *Uriposia*, the drinking of urine, *hemoposia*, the drinking of blood. Words like this rise up like small dead things, gleaming sickly white, in the middle of the night. I hang on to them once I've found them in books, and even though they are dead, they buoy me up. They are better than the smothering nothing I nudged up against for the first couple of months. Better than the vision that troubles me now, blindsiding me with its uselessness. I know the end of the story, always the end of the story, though it's no good to anyone now. At first, the visions were fractured: the blinding glare of headlights, Quill turning her face away as though she saw it coming. Always she dove down deeper in the lake than anyone else. And always she returned, grinning and squinting in the sun, shivering as I wrapped a towel around her.

"Where've you been," I asked.

"To the other side of the world," she said. "You should see it, Mom. I love it down there."

"In my dreams, sweet pea. You know I'm not a swimmer."

But I never dreamt of water, only rain.

In the winter, we slept till after nine, the light easing to silver, then brightening through the white lace curtains in our bedroom like radioactive milk.

Quill, even as a toddler, would be awake before me. Perhaps she and her father enjoyed some private moment or maybe it was only the sound of Michael stoking up the wood furnace in the cellar before he left in the dark that woke her.

When I opened my eyes, she would be lying beside me. Pale brown eyes large in her small face just starting to lengthen. The pillow sank beneath her so that it suddenly occurred to me that her head had weight, was full of her own thoughts.

I yawned and put my arm across her small shoulders.

"What are you looking at, Quill?"

"I'm watching you dream," she said.

"How do you know I'm dreaming?"

"I can see," she said and looked at the ceiling. "Up there. There were trees across the road. They fell down."

And she was right. It was a dream I had before when I was pregnant with her. The black skies opened in a torrent of rain and the prairie ground started to shift, slipping and sliding into impossible mud. The shallow roots of poplars lining the narrow roads were losing their grip and toppled with gusts of wind.

How this terrified me the first time it really happened. It had rained all night. The air, usually gritty in my nose, was thick, smelling of tears — the salt in the soil dissolving into the wet air. Michael could hardly wait to get the four-wheel drive started.

"Put your seatbelt on. We're going for a ride." Though he didn't fasten his own. He slid the truck from shoulder to shoulder, leaving yellow ruts in the mud behind us. We rounded the curve and slid suddenly sideways when he saw the poplar across the road.

I dreamt this over and over, trees losing their footing both before and behind us on this land where nothing could be predicted. Where roads could be even more impassable in summer than in winter. So Michael brought me a name from the back-to-the-land community near Willow Lake.

"If Mohammed cannot go to the mountain, then the mountain will come to Mohammed," he said.

The dreams stopped once the midwife arrived. Jessie, with her light brown hair springing from the red scarf she tied at the back of her neck, with her good soups and backrubs and easy prophesies.

"This is a strong baby — a strong heart," she said, with the stethoscope pressed against my belly. "This one wants to be alive."

Just before labour started, Michael and I sat in the truck at four in the morning down near the community pasture. He had a beer balanced between his thighs. The baby was so big, I felt like someone was sitting on my knee — a feeling I remembered from my teens, when too many of us would pile into a car. The suffocation of breathing into someone's back, unable to see. But this presence, even with the weight, was still a phantom and I could see clearly the brush piles of fire across the newly cleared field. Orange flickered and sprayed up in jets of sparks when the breeze lifted, lighting Michael's face with a weird rapt intensity. For weeks, these fires smoldered by day and flickered by night, like northern lights suddenly hot and snagged in these rough piles of poplar. The more prosperous farmers had bought up old fields left fallow, were reclaiming them from rough bush that had grown up, bulldozing trees into long piles and letting fire do most of the work. Through those nights in August, we could see the glow in the sky from three sides and it often drew us out when we couldn't sleep. We felt protected by a ring of fire.

It seemed prophetic, the way it started, a sudden soaking gush of salty warmth beneath me as we watched the fire. It seemed like fire and water would always mix. We would be blessed for life.

Michael rocks against me in his sleep. It's a sea-sickening feeling, his neediness, his radar even when he's unconscious so powerful his body would know if I turned towards him. He would envelop me in an instant. Thirst gets me out of bed, draws me parched towards the bathroom sink stained with northern water. The water here is drawn to the surface so painfully, it's tinged with blood. And it stinks. When I first came here from the city to live with him, he tasted like it. His kiss seemed like the kiss of an impostor; someone who looked like him and talked like him but wasn't really him. He noticed my shyness, so I laughed and told him he had abducted the real Michael.

"It's the water. What's the human body, 98% water? Give yourself a few weeks and every cell will fill up and you won't notice a thing. Your skin," and he kissed my forehead. "Your brain will fill up and all you'll want is sex, day and night."

"Don't you wish."

"Your breasts will fill up," and he started to undo the top buttons of my shirt. This was the first inkling that I had come here more than temporarily, the first hint of Quill's possible existence.

He is again a stranger, and I stand with a glass of tinged water in my hand unable to drink. I've forgotten how. The muscles in my throat tense, my breathing comes in ragged bursts. I can only drink in sips over many hours. The simple rhythmic pleasure is gone. Yet I'm always thirsty.

For the longest time I left the first and last postcard she ever sent us up on the fridge. On the way to Edmonton to visit the West Edmonton Mall, the schoolbus stopped in Vegreville for lunch, near the giant Ukrainian painted egg. On the front is the egg, intricate with bright designs, tilted a little to the side against an intense blue sky. Her message is half printed, half written.

"This egg is as big as a dinosaur! As big as the whole world! I love you. Quill." Her name is cursive, slanted a little like the egg, with just glimmerings of the person she will become, the dashing, slanted hand of a woman on the move. There is an eraser smudge on the word "whole" and I can see beneath it that she had originally written "hole."

The card arrived the week we buried her in the little Turtle Lake cemetery. I didn't get out of the car. The dirt heaped in the snow looked obscene, looked like a pile of shit. Michael grabbed my leg just above the knee, hard, said: "We've got to. We owe it to her."

"No. You go."

"And if I don't, who does?"

I didn't answer. There were other people there but we couldn't see them. It was as though the people around us had died and become the ghosts while Quill was still very real. And for me, it stayed that way. Ghost faces, ghost friends, ghost family calling long-distance. By then, our breath had frozen on the inside of the glass of the minister's car. I couldn't see the pile of shit anymore. But I heard frozen dirt viciously rattle on the top of her box, and then a heavier sound as the earth filled in, a dull thud like the sound of geese shot in flight hitting the ground.

Michael didn't see it through either. He came back to the car, the shape of him blurry and dark against the silvery frost of the windows, coming closer, holding it all inside until he closed the car door. That heaving grief, like being sick. I floated up inside my head, wanting to drift up into the cold cold blue.

"You wanted her to go to school," I said. "I could have taught her at home, but you wanted her to go to school."

I went to the minister's church once more after. I sat at the back so that the sunlight cutting through the clear narrow windows like a knife wouldn't fall on me. No stained glass here, no colour to soften the long prairie winter. Just relentless light, making me see everything too clearly. A few Indian grandmothers sat near me with purple kerchiefs over their hair. One smiled slightly and nodded her head as I slipped into the pew beside her. They know what it's like. Children are always dying out on the reserve, in house fires, by carbon monoxide in cars stuck in snowdrifts. I hear these things, and carry them around with me, as they must carry my loss around with them. I lie in bed making comparisons, as though shopping for a more bearable kind of grief.

Everyone in the church was old. The white women all sat in front of me, their hair white, silver and variations on blue. They wore little fur hats on their heads. They went all the way to Saskatoon for these hats, years ago, just after the war. They wouldn't know what to do if someone from the reserve placed the bloody skins in their hands fresh from the trap.

The gospel was from Matthew. An angel appears to Joseph in a dream and tells him to flee to Egypt because Herod is about to search for the child and destroy him. In his anger at their escape, Herod kills all the male children two years of age and younger. I'd heard enough. I got up to leave. Then I heard my name. God was speaking to me, but I will not listen. I would have listened then. He could have warned me. But not now. Not ever again.

In the morning, Michael is gone, where I do not know. What is out of sight is a welcome blank. Once, late last winter, he almost made me see what I could not see. He arrived at dawn, opened the bedroom door before I heard his truck. He had been walking all night, all the way from Turtle Lake. His truck was marooned out in the snow on the frozen lake. He slipped into bed beside me, still wrapped in the metallic smell of fresh cold, and put his arms around me, his chest against me making me shiver. He told me the moonlight was so beautiful on the snow of the lake that he revved the truck, took a run at it, and sailed far out into the fluffy track-less snow. It sprayed up around him sparkling, bouncing off his windshield before he came to rest twenty yards from shore.

"You know what, Rachel? It was worth it." And for a moment I saw the light lifting in little sharp points from the night, and the lake spread out before me pristine and unbroken, something of the possibility of beauty in the world without her. But I turned over, told him to plug in the old Volvo, to drive over to Hurdman's farm for the tractor. I didn't want to go with him. He got here on his own. He could go back alone for all I cared.

I lie in bed smoking, watching it curl into vague flowers in the air above me. The fluted shape of blue lilies blooming, wilting and fading in the air. I slip down low in the bed and see what isn't. What is, what was, I had to leave behind. The Sands Hotel, which we never saw. Quill caught by her bathing suit on the drain at the bottom of the hotel pool. I used to see her thrashing, the legs of the others far above her, near light. I used to see her taking those first lungfuls of water, relaxing a little because she can breathe as she did before she was born. A miracle, she can breathe under water, and she can hardly wait to tell me about this amazing thing that happened to her. But there are no miracles. God is silent. I'm waiting for her, but the future is tainted by the past. I can't keep it from happening.

*

Quill and her husband and their six-year-old boy are traveling in the desert. They are driving a Volvo through Egypt, out into the Sahara. She likes the feeling of moving out into extremity. Never has she felt more alive. The sand around them is braided and harder than she would have thought. Her teeth rattle in her head when they hit a ripple broadwise. Her son is in the backseat where I cannot see him clearly. I only know her love for him as part of the great heart-line passed from mother to child, from me to him through her. Her husband is gentle, a rough-looking gypsy who cherishes her. A man much like her father.

He says to her: "Why don't you drive for awhile. I'm getting sleepy." This is well past the turn of the millennium. The desert hasn't changed, will never change. If anything, it has gathered its forces, its ancient Biblical forces, and has smothered small village oases, date palm groves, dissolving mud houses back into a nothingness and driving people back into war with their neighbours. Far beneath the surface are aquifers full of fossil water, from the time when seas covered this continent. Quill feels the presence of these waters in her blood, sees their waves floating above the surface of the horizon.

"Sure," she says. "Do I look out for markers?"

"Just follow the tracks and we should cross the border by dawn."

Their son is already asleep and Quill slows down so he isn't jarred awake. Wood bangles she bought in the market in Alexandria slide down her forearm creating a warm hollow music as he and his father sleep. The mischievous pointed face I know so well has molded into a face more feral and wise. The sun sinks quickly, lighting up the drifts of sand and hard rock golden-orange, sinking to rose like a fire deepening its embers. Blue slides up from the other horizon and it is suddenly dark. Quill stops the car to step out into the air, filling her lungs. It feels like drinking cool water. Stars float to the surface of the sky in torrents above her. The suddenness of it makes her a bit faint. She thinks of that old-fashioned word *swoon*. She's swooning with the beauty of the desert at night. She's thankful to be alive.

She drives all night on the braided tracks. Now and then she feels a soft sinking feeling under the car, she drifts a little sideways as in a boat, but manages to find hard ground again and carries on. The braided tracks are caused by other vehicles bogged down in sand. People swerve to get around them and the pattern continues for what looks like infinity. She's been told the braided tracks are ten miles wide in places.

He wakes near dawn, a pale whitish-rose lid lifting in the east, and behind it the fierce sun, fierce witness of everything that moves below. The sun's attention is too much. He checks maps.

"Did you see a line of rocky cliffs off to your right?"

"We've passed so many rocks," she says. Their son wakes and tells them he needs to pee. They both hold each other back, tense, as they watch his clear water seep into the sand and disappear. They want to tell him to try to hold it back; they wonder if they should have found an empty canteen to save it, but they're not yet ready to admit what they each know.

"C'mon hon. The sun's hot. Back in the car," Quill says. She passes him an orange, some dates and unleavened bread in the back-seat. He eats, gazing out the tinted window, still half-claimed by his dream of a narrow country road lined with poplar, throwing a red ball for a black dog. Dreams of home. Dreams of me at the door calling his name. "Ishmael. Ishmael, aren't you cold yet?" my voice carrying across the snow.

When the sun is highest in the sky, they run out of gas. They sit silently in the car until the heat drives them out into the desert, and then under the car in a shallow dugout where there is at least shade. Quill squints as she does when calling her long-distance vision into being. It's an expression I've seen often; lifting her sharp chin slightly as though she's sniffing something on the breeze. She waits for a glint on a windshield.

Their son begins to cry near sundown.

"Izzy, it's really important that you be strong and not cry. OK?" Quill says, putting her arm around him, her mouth to his cheek. She tastes his tears and keeps her mouth there until he's stopped. Then she realizes what she has been doing. She's a ghoul, not a mother, she thinks.

When the water runs out, she gives him his own urine to drink and as much of hers as he can take.

"Yours is too strong for him," she tells her husband. "Keep your own strength up. I'm going to need you."

"Then you have it," he says, holding out his jar of dark yellow fluid.

"No, you," Quill says, pushing it back.

"Please, I don't care about me. He needs you."

"Male pee stinks. What do you put in the stuff?"

"We're way past gourmet here," he says. They push the jar back and forth till they finally laugh. Quill's heart beats quick and hard. She knows it is the last laugh they will ever share.

On the third day, he digs a trench below the engine, moving slowly because they are so fatigued. He brings back radiator coolant in a clear glass jar, bright green, which makes her head hurt just looking at it. The fluid seems to gel in the hot sun, like green blood, but it's just an illusion.

"It's not so bad," she tells him, taking her first mouthful.

Still she thinks it's just as well that their son is beyond drinking now. He lies in the shallow bowl of sand under the car breathing fast, his skin thinning like an old man's. She sits beside him, stroking his forehead. For awhile, he whined and tried to sweep her hand away, but he no longer makes a sound.

Talking is difficult now for her too. But she says to her husband: "This is familiar somehow. I've been here before."

"No. We would never have come back," her husband says. "If only we'd known."

"But I know this place. I've done this before. I swear."

Their son hallucinates. He tries to cry out, but his voice crackles and clicks in his throat. His tongue is swelling. How she does it, or exactly when, she doesn't record. She writes on maps, first on the edges and borders to preserve them, then on top of lines and little points of settlements when it doesn't matter anymore. I will be given these maps. After many months, or maybe years, I will find them in my hands.

"He's out of pain. I feel nothing," she writes.

She's alone now. After they stop their son's breathing and cover him with silky sand, her husband lifts his wrist to her, tells her, "Drink. You still have a chance." And to her shame, she does, through a slit he's made in his forearm, but the blood doesn't flow fast enough. It is so thick. So he holds his chin up as he lies beside her and she cuts through and drinks from his neck. Before he has even stopped breathing, she throws up red in the sand. It dries quickly and is lifted by the wind, mixed with thousands of grains of sand.

"I don't regret coming here," she writes. "The desert is so powerful, so beautiful. I only regret it's not an easier death, a soothing death, cool and soothing. I long to drown."

*

And I'm back where I begin. The package of cigarettes is empty, so I rise. I put my parka on over my housecoat and go outside to the chicken coop we fashioned from an old garden shed. The air is so cold, I gasp, then reach down to zip up the front and find gloves in my pockets. My eyes are watering, then quickly freeze so that my eyelashes are sealed together by this flashing line of ice.

Inside the coop is that musty smell that hints of summer. The hens are on their perches, dark feathers puffed up, heads tucked under flightless wings. Their quiet female broodiness used to be such a comfort to me, but now they feel like a reproach. Quill loved them, especially when we first brought them home, peeping in a box, growing in the dark under blood-red lights.

"Can I sit with them here, Mom?"

"Sit too long under this magic light and you'll start laying eggs," I told her, struck by the sudden picture of her with her own child someday.

I reach into box after box of straw, sweep around with my gloved hand, finding nothing. This is not a choice I make, but a kind of certainty I answer to. I step out into the fenced-in chicken-run, clear off the wide stump, open our little tool-shed and find what I need.

I choose the one first furthest from the door. The bird quivers warm in my hands, a few misfired impulses to fly, then it settles in against my stomach. Once we reach the light, I grab its feet, swing it out in front of me the way I've seen Michael do and with one quick arc of axe on wood, its head falls to the ground. The hen jerks out of my hands, beating wings convulsively, making thin trails of blood, looping like handwriting in the snow.

I go back for the next and the next. They don't see it coming. It's not part of their winter vocabulary. It's so cold, blood freezes like glue on my cheek, freezes into little pellets underfoot. I throw the hens' bodies in a small pile. This is not very well planned. The pot should be boiling so that they can be dipped and the dark feathers come clean from the shocking white flesh.

Arms clamp me from behind. The axe-head brushes my boot.

"You've snapped. You've really snapped," Michael shouts in my ear. I can't get loose so I try to bite his arm. His jacket is too thick.

"Are you ready to stop now?" And he flings me away from him.

I've come to rest close to the chickens. The feathers ruffle slightly in the air, but it's all surface motion. The birds are inert as brown stones.

"Why don't you just tear out my heart? Will that be enough blood shed for you?" He's baiting me, fueled by a hate I recognize as his unshakable will to survive.

The word floats up from the carnage. "*Hemoposia*," I say and a raw giggle breaks through to the surface.

"What?"

"I did this. It's something," I tell him.

Then he's suddenly crying. He sits back in the snow with his head forward.

We prepared the chickens together. We went through the motions of salvaging something from the morning. When it's a larger animal, like a moose or deer, it's called dressing the animal. In fact, we were stripping something once living down to meat and bone. Feathers off, cavities ripped clean, washed inside and out so no blood stains the flesh. He was no longer angry. We stood, hips almost touching at the counter. I dipped the bodies in boiling water, held them for a minute, then lifted them out to pluck them on newspaper.

Usually we do this outside in the summer after he has killed them, and you get some distance and distraction from the details. I tore out handfuls of feathers, shook them into a garbage bag. They stuck, soft and cloying, to my wet hands. Then he gutted the birds, cutting both ends with his knife, pulling out the tough insides. I kept my eyes averted from the strange greens and purples of glistening organs, the smell, humid as sex, wafting up between us.

"It's OK, Rachel. They don't feel a thing now."

Then he passed them back to me for rinsing and plucking of the last stubborn shafts of feathers from around the legs and low on the belly. This familiar act, passing their bodies warm and yielding from hand to hand, like washing a newborn.

"Quills," I said. He kept working, but I sensed a pause, a holding of breath. Then, quietly I said her name.

"Do you ever wonder?" I asked him.

He was cautious. He looked at me sideways, sizing up what I wanted from him.

"Wonder how they touched her? Did they even know her name?" I said.

"I don't know what you mean," he said.

"She was naked at the hospital. Who took off her bathing suit? Was it when she was being saved or when they'd given up?"

"The nurse maybe. She was crying, remember?"

"What was she wearing, what did she wear in the coffin?"

He paused, then answered.

"I bought her a dress in town. I went to buy a dress, but they gave it to me. It was plaid, Blackwatch I think. And Iris from the reserve gave me moccasins, for her journey she said."

"Thank you, Michael. I don't remember a thing, except that her hair was dry. Not a mark on her. It didn't make sense."

"No, it doesn't."

When we were close to done, Michael said he needed to clear his head. He's cutting wood in the clearing in the forest north of the house, like he always does this time of year. The trees are junk trees really, just new growth poplar and some birch taking over the poorer fields not cultivated since the Thirties when everyone from the south moved up here to avoid the drought. Now there are ghost houses all over. Most people didn't put their roots down. They built quick slanting houses, like the one we live in now, then walked away when their real home, their real fields came back to life after the dust settled.

But Michael loves this land and everything about it. Sometimes he puts his chainsaw down and leans against the cold grey skin of a poplar, looking up at the sky, swaying the tree with his body. Sometimes he just chops at the base of a tree with great swinging blows of his axe, grunting like a tennis player or Olympic rower. I've seen him do these things when I've come upon him unexpectedly, when Quill and I used to take afternoon walks in the forest. He would look surprised and come over to us, lifting Quill in his arms. He usually had something wonderful to show her: the place where deer had slept, flattening the grass, a wasp's nest high in a tree, coyote tracks along the creek.

It's the feeling that he's out there somewhere holding her in his arms that has me pulling on my boots, finding my hat and down-filled mitts and pulling on my parka, still smeared with chicken blood. The sun and cold slap me in the face but instead of waking me up, the blow makes me feel a little dazed, as though the past year may not have really happened and she's out there. But it's too cold. He never would have brought a child with him to cut wood in February. This is the first time I've had this sense, this release from her terrible absence.

I turn away from the prairie into the bush and hear a dry creaking of wood as two branches scrape together over my head. The air is so cold, it is almost electric, so cold it almost feels like intense heat, and I wouldn't be surprised if the bare tree tops burst into flames. I walk by the frozen slough and imagine the frogs frozen solid. Not even the core of the earth is warm enough to touch them. And Quill, I do not imagine her physical form now, knowing through the whole restless seething summer that she had entered the cycle of life in a terrible way, life making use of her, carrying her further and further away from me. It's easier now that she, too, is frozen, held in a pause.

The clearing is ahead of me, out in open air. The light seems a little more fierce. My forehead is starting to pound from the cold. I don't hear the chainsaw. There is silence. Still, I know he's here. Something led me here, something that fills me with calm.

I find him across the clearing, inside the ring of trees. There is a dark shape almost invisible, like the first warmth of spring that melts in rings around the base of trees so that you know there really is life down there, no matter how cold it's been, and no matter how long the winter has lasted. Something too warm to stay covered by snow. There are his boot-prints all through the clearing, looping in circles, grinding sawdust into the ground. I could trace his steps and find out where he's been, in what order and how this happened, but it's random really. It makes no difference. There are tangles of branches from the high tops of poplar trees, silvery as steel wool. He seems to be very still but as I get closer I see that he's shivering violently and the skin around his eyes and mouth is blue.

I've had to step through the fallen crown of a tree to reach him where he lies pinned under the branches and upper trunk. The bark is torn and shredded above him. At first I think he has done this with his bare hands, with his nails, but then I notice the axe beside him.

He doesn't seem to realize I'm here. I free the axe, drawing it up from below branches and hack away some of the smaller ones that keep me from reaching him. Then I find the reserve of strength inside me and somehow lift the tree, letting it fall beside him. He opens his eyes but doesn't seem to recognize me.

I unzip his parka. He turns his head away. He will not look me in the eye, no matter what I bring. He made his choice after Quill. I make mine now. I open my coat, lie down on top of him, curling his arms inward so that his hands are locked under my arms, chest to chest, his heart is beating too fast. His shivers almost shake me off and after awhile he winces.

"My lungs," he says, quiet, a higher tone in his voice, like the tone he will have as an old man. "I think I've collapsed a lung."

I shift so that my weight is lower. The colour slowly changes in his face. I'm eager for it, thirsty for it, watch for blood rising from his heart. We lie like this for a long time, my tears freezing on my face, before I can help him home.

First Flame

BY NADINE MCINNIS

At a certain age,
all girls nourish a small flame in their rooms,
a sharp tongue of blue wavering like a reflection in a mirror.

It flickers, forked, and their hearts quicken
to the electrical charge of a snipped thread of lightning.

She only watches it at first.
It has nothing to do with her, just a storm
flaring blue sheets over a town beyond the horizon.

Someday she will live in that town
under the throbbing sky and the wind will press
her damp clothes against her breasts, pushing her down,
and every cell in her body will ionize for him.

There may be roofs torn by a headstrong wind.
There may be children left homeless,
fire running along all the overhead wires, brief flashing explosions
and fragments of milky glass piercing petals in the wrecked gardens.

But for now, there is only this small flame cupped in glass,
and her shadow
cast huge and quivering on the wall.

The day will come when you tell her
you don't want her burning candles in her room
and she'll walk right past you as though she hasn't heard,
drifting down the basement stairs silent as smoke.

Mothers remember the seduction of struck sulphur,
the grit and sizzle of it, the heady whiff,
and how easy it is to fall asleep as candle flame nudges the window
sending out its beacon to any man passing by below.

They know that soon enough
there will be that fuse lit between the legs, a bright flash
tearing her open in a fiery thread.

But the girls warming their hands over their futures
sit rapt around their small fires,

knowing that the Celts were right so long ago
when they gathered all their kin on a hilltop
on the longest night of the year, and sent a virgin
alone to light the first hearth fire in the darkened village.

The girls are sure and patient as the nights thicken.
They wait and watch the flame curve to the life force
exhaled, inhaled in their own soft chests.

This is the light they breathe, the light they will touch
when they carry it back into the world.

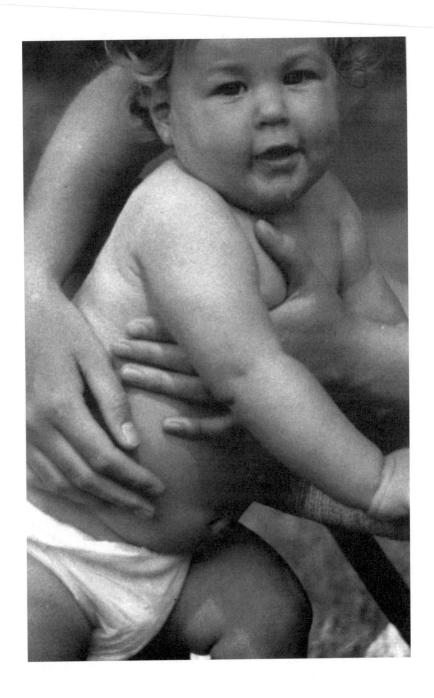

Carmen Waits

BY SUSAN ZETTELL

Carmen sits by the window and watches hummingbirds fight. Crystalline autumn light defines her sharp nose, the cleft in her chin, illuminates her wide-set eyes. Glints off the brassy iridescence of the hummingbirds' bodies. When she tires of their fighting she looks over at her husband, Ron. Sometimes she looks down at the floor because she thinks she sees an insect skitter across the shiny hardwood. When she turns her head it is gone.

"Did you see that?" she asks Ron who is reading a mystery novel, his favourite kind next to westerns.

"What?" he asks, but he doesn't look up, doesn't look Carmen in the eye.

Carmen has been seeing insects at the periphery of her vision all her life. Even before her mother died and Carmen went crazy. *Situational depression*, Carmen's psychiatrist told her, coaxing her to talk, tidying up her craziness, normalizing and encapsulating her grief in two precise clinical words. As if she cared. The situation had been death. The depression the hollow on the mattress where the weight of her mother's body had rested for the months of her illness. The depression into which Carmen curled herself the day after her mother's funeral, where Carmen lay until her father lifted her from her mother's bed to take her to be cured.

Carmen had stopped washing, stopped eating, stopped getting up in the morning. Carmen had stopped her periods from coming. She had stopped talking. Some days she was afraid of the rug beside the bed; some days, when she watched the curtains as they billowed on a gentle breeze coming in through the window, Carmen was sure she would die of fear. One day terror came when she saw the doorknob to the bedroom door turn. It was not that she was afraid of someone coming in; she was simply terrified of the doorknob. She didn't tell anyone about being afraid. She didn't tell anyone anything.

On the morning he took her to the psychiatrist, her father lifted her from the pungent wrinkled caress of the sheets. He carried her to a waiting bath, gently placed her in it, nightgown and all. Then he left her, and Carmen's Auntie Norma, her mother's sister, came in to bathe her, lifting the thin wet nightgown over Carmen's head, scrubbing her like a child, washing her hair with baby shampoo that did not sting her eyes.

"Oh my scrawny sad bird," her auntie crooned. "You're just a handful of bones."

Her auntie poured water over her shoulders. "Come back, Carmen."

Carmen watched her auntie's competent hands, so like her mother's, thick soft white fingers, each almost as wide as it was long, square-cut fingernails painted the red of a hummingbird's throat. Ruby red. Or she watched her auntie's lips, two small bright flapping wings beating out sounds that were all the same to Carmen. *Hum, hum, hum. Hum, hum, hum.*

In her head Carmen knew she loved her auntie, loved her father as he carried her out to the car, drove her to the psychiatrist's office. In her heart she felt nothing at all.

Carmen has never told anyone that she sees insects out of the corner of her eye. Especially not Ron. He has begun to think Carmen lives her life on shaky ground. She doesn't want to encourage his thoughts too much. Until the pregnancy she felt protected with Ron, safe. Now she finds herself provoking him in small ways, like the zipper shoes she bought yesterday.

Carmen likes zippers. On anything, but especially on leather. The shoes are a nappy brushed black leather. They look like Hush Puppies with thick square three-inch black rubber heels that make her taller than Ron, who is five-foot-five. They have shiny wide stainless steel zippers up the front.

Carmen tried the shoes on four separate times before she bought them. They pinched a bit. Nothing she couldn't stand until they were broken in. They were one hundred and two dollars without tax. But no, those weren't the reasons she hesitated. It was the fact that Ron would hate them. In the end she tried to please him by buying him a new copy of his favourite western, *Lonesome Dove*, when she finally bought the shoes.

"I have *Lonesome Dove*," he said.

"It's falling apart. There are elastics around it."

"I like it like that," he said.

"Why don't you like them?"

"I didn't say that."

"Ron," Carmen said.

"They're ugly. Why do you do it?"

"What?" Carmen asked.

"Make yourself look hard. They're slutty."

"That's what I like about them, Ron."

Carmen wears the shoes now with a sweater she bought that is the colour of illness. It, too, has a zipper. She got the sweater on sale. The zipper runs on a slant, but it shouldn't. Defective, but Carmen doesn't mind.

The sunlight from the window warms a spot on her belly. Carmen rubs it, caresses the warmed flesh beneath her sweater. She would like to whisper to the baby, ask it to stay, ask it why it is threatening to come too soon. Perhaps it is defective, too. Perhaps that is why.

Sometimes the flitting shadows Carmen sees are bigger than insects, but she doesn't want to think about that. Insects are manageable. She is not particularly afraid of insects though she prefers not to have to deal with centipedes or spiders with hairy bodies. House spiders are fine. Ron makes her leave them alone.

"Don't kill spiders," he tells her when she gets a tissue to whisk a transparent winter spider into the toilet, "It'll rain. And they eat bugs."

Carmen doesn't point out that it's winter and unlikely to rain, or that there are no bugs in the house except for these pale thin spiders that move slowly, almost invisibly, across her walls. Because there *are* insects. Even if Ron can't see them. Instead she gently wraps the spider inside a tissue and carries it to the basement where she releases it, knowing that soon it will make its way back upstairs to its proper home.

Carmen doesn't like the cobwebs spiders leave. But once, over five warm spring days, Carmen watched a huge black spider build and rebuild a perfect glittering web between the stems of the plants in her garden. The spider's body was two inches long, hairy, with yellow stripes across its back. It carried an oversized woven egg sac at the base of its abdomen.

The web was strong enough to catch wasps and bumble bees, and one day a beetle the size of a quarter. The spider did not bother Carmen, but then it wasn't slipping past her on the floor faster than she could see, hidden from view by a lash or the blink of an eye. On the sixth day the spider was gone, its web a tattered fragment drifting on a breeze. Later that day Carmen watched as a pair of hummingbirds took strand after strand of the spider's silk to decorate their nest.

The spider had deserted the web before her eggs had hatched. It reminded Carmen of her mother leaving one day for an ultrasound to confirm an embarrassing, but exciting, unexpected, late-in-life pregnancy: no period, extreme tiredness, an abdomen that was growing rounder, more distended. She only came home to die. The pregnancy turned out to be a tumour. Her mother died within five months. Carmen was fourteen.

That's when Carmen decided she'd never have a baby. But then she changed her mind.

"Are you going to have it?" Ron wanted to know.

"Yes."

"I'm fifty-two," Ron said.

"I'm thirty-seven."

"You could have an abortion," Ron told her.

"I planned it".

"You said you never wanted to have children."

"I changed my mind, Ron," Carmen said.

Carmen met Ron at a university lecture, by the eminent orthopedic surgeon, Matthew Frenton, on "Alignment: The Use of Computers and Carpal Tunnel Syndrome." The lecture had been extremely technical and only two people asked questions afterwards: Carmen Lescombe, Student,

Kinesiology and Dr. Ronald Patrickson, Neurologist. That evening Ron asked Carmen to have supper with him.

Ron was thirty-seven, recently divorced. Carmen was twenty-two. After supper Carmen slept with Ron. Because she was twenty-two and why not. Because he made her laugh. Because he had a gentle smiling mouth and kisses as soft and comforting as white bread. *But that's it*, she told him, *once and no more*. She didn't want anything serious, didn't want a middle-aged man on the rebound.

In the morning Carmen awoke to the sound of water running. Ron came into the bedroom, lifted Carmen from the bed and carried her to the bathroom where he lowered her, naked, into the water. He washed her like a child; shampooed her hair, massaged her scalp until she groaned with pleasure. He didn't get soap in her eyes.

Carmen had taken psychology; she'd read about Freud. Ron talked to her while he bathed her and all she heard was a pretty hum. *Hum, hum, hum.* While her body relaxed, inside her head Carmen was alert and wary. Yes, she'd read in textbooks about girls falling in love with older men, their fathers. And Carmen had to admit she felt slightly stupid, slightly embarrassed.

In her heart Carmen felt almost nothing. Not happiness. Not unhappiness. But she did feel safe.

"I don't have children. I never want to have children," Ron told Carmen at supper the night before.

"Neither do I," Carmen had said.

As far as Carmen knew that was the truth for she had already had an abortion. When she was twenty-one, five months before she met Ron. The baby partly belonged to Bernie Sanderson, who said he loved Carmen until she told him she was pregnant. Not that she loved Bernie Sanderson, or wanted to have his baby, but she did want Bernie to come to Boston with her when she went for the abortion.

Bernie had fleshy brutal lips and teeth that left faint bruises on Carmen's skin. She had been studying too hard that term, and working at a part-time job she didn't much like. She was always tired. Bernie's biting kisses kept her awake, or at least alert to the possibility of pleasure.

Carmen flew to Boston alone and was surprised, upon landing, by spring, the thick smell of it — decaying leaf mold, thawed dog shit, warming soil. Greenery bursting, bulbs already fading, tulips on stems too tall, leaning, precarious. Shedding petals like bits of old skin. It made her cry, this shock of spring, when what she'd left behind was a frigid bright late winter day, mounds of sand and salt-discoloured snow, and the cold heart of a young man with greedy, cruel lips.

Carmen didn't tell anyone where she had gone. She spent all her savings on the flight and the abortion, paid cash, went straight back to classes the morning after her return. As if nothing happened. But Carmen remembered her friend, Sandra, from high school, remembered when Sandra had had an abortion during their last term. Sandra left her hospital bracelet in her underwear drawer, right on top, where Sandra's mother discovered it on laundry day.

Sandra told Carmen that her mother called the principal's office and had Sandra sent home, due to a family emergency, her mother had said, which is what Sandra was told. *Go straight home, there is a family emergency.* When Sandra got home her mother took her in her arms and cried. *My poor darling,* she said over and over until Sandra realized her mother was crying for her.

Carmen felt, if she couldn't have the kind of sympathy Sandra had, she wanted no sympathy at all.

The reason Carmen changed her mind about a baby had to do with a dream. Until the dream, Carmen remembered her mother as she looked when she was dying: shrunken, hair as short as an air force cadet's, skin so bruised and tight and thin it looked as if it would split if Carmen touched it. So she didn't. Her mother's hands, once so wide and effective, picked at the sheets of the bed. Sometimes her mother gasped for breath, fish-like, lips opening and closing, useless, cracked and glistening with the vaseline Carmen's father dabbed on them.

Just die, Carmen wanted to say, but instead she said, "Mama, don't leave me. Please."

In the dream Carmen and her mother are exactly the same age. And her mother is healthy, vibrant, her hair and eyes shining, snapping electrically, her skin thick and radiant as an autumn apple's, blushing. Her lips are full and soft, moist and smiling.

Carmen stands to greet her mother who approaches her, comes closer and closer until her mother touches her, is upon her, then enters her, becomes her. Her arms are Carmen's arms, her hair, her lips, her smile are Carmen's. Together they hum with energy, sparkle, laugh and laugh and laugh because they are so beautiful, so alive.

When Carmen awoke, still laughing, she turned to Ron, aroused him, and made love to him. Carmen was fertile, could feel it, had been waiting for the moment even as she had denied it. She wanted, alive in her, whatever bits of her mother she already carried. She wanted to see those bits with her own eyes: a mouth, a gesture, the shape of a finger-nail, perhaps the gentle indentation where the ankle curves to meet the heel.

Now Carmen sits in her chair by the window, this clear fall light so pure and pretty it makes her want to cry.

This morning Carmen had an ultrasound and she remembers every word of the report:

Large intra-uterine gestational sac measuring 2.2 X 2.1 cm.
Tiny fetal pole with crown-rump length of 0.4 cm. in keeping
with a 5 week pregnancy. Sac suggests an 8 week pregnancy.
There is a very slow heartbeat.
There is a small implantation bleed.
Opinion: The size of the intra-uterine gestational sac is larger
than one would expect for a crown-rump length of 0.4 cm. There
is a very slow heartbeat. A miscarriage may be imminent.

"The good news is that there *is* a fetal heartbeat," Dr. McAdam told Carmen. "That's encouraging." Dr. McAdam had pink lipstick on her teeth. "Now go home and put your feet up, Carmen. Wait and see. There's nothing you can do."

The dream sustains her. Carmen wills this baby to survive, wills it to hold to her. Wills her blood push through the thick blue braided cord of the umbilicus straight into her baby's slowly beating heart.

Carmen sits in her maroon chair by the window watching two vicious jade-green hummingbirds fight. Autumn light, sharp and lumi-nous and blue, glints off the zippers of her brushed black leather shoes. Like a queen, her feet are raised on a carved footstool. Her gentle hus-band, Ron, rubs his forehead as he reads his mystery novel. He cannot meet Carmen's eye.

Carmen waits. And sometimes she thinks she can see an insect dart across her shiny cold hardwood floor. There goes one now.

Facts About Niagara

BY SUSAN ZETTELL

"When one stands near the Falls and looks down, one is seized with Horror, and the Head turns round, so that one cannot look long or steadfastly upon it."

Father Louis Hennepin, 1683

Resistance was impossible. It was too late. Already Georgina's vision had blurred, her sense of smell had abated. Taste, unnecessary and frivolous, had dissolved. Hearing remained, though as aqueous, submerged echoes. External touch was superfluous; all essential sensation eddied within her.

Her heart, forgotten at her core, became the pulse of her pain, its coursing courier. Breath burst from her lungs, deluges of grunts and gasps, propelled by each crashing spasm, each rushing, rhythmical, unstoppable torrent of agony.

Georgina, drowned in misery, embraced it, became a swelling blissful cataract of pain. She was affliction; she was torment. She was this scream, this fearsome, wild, unending wail.

Until Christopher was born.

*

Georgina surfaces from her memory of Christopher's birth exactly twenty years ago. 11:21 a.m. She looks up from her desk and watches her mother, Constance Voll, take off her coat and gently place it on the rack. Her mother is tall and trim. Erect. Her fine colourless hair, deeply parted on the right then combed severely to the left, hangs at an angle that is straight as a ruler just below her tiny fine-boned ears.

But when her mother smiles, as she is now, all the lines on her face appear round and happy.

"Hello Constance," Georgina says. From the time Georgina was learning to speak, she was forbidden to call her mother anything but Constance. Georgina smiles back at her mother, and her smile, like her mother's, is generous, seems wide and convincing.

Constance retired two years ago from her job as a veterinarian's assistant, a career she had before she married, and kept, with one vet or another, until her retirement. "I'm a working gal," her mother always said, "Never much liked the domestic arts." Georgina's father did all of the laundry and cleaning after work, bought groceries every Saturday morning taking with him the coupons he'd clipped from newspapers and flyers.

He made arrangements for Georgina to attend an infant day nursery when Georgina was seven months old. He bathed her, read to her, kissed her goodnight and tucked her in. Then her mother would come to the door, stand a moment, book in hand, her finger marking her place. She'd turn out the light. "'Night, Georgina," she'd say and blow a kiss.

Her father did all of the cooking though there were seven dishes for which Constance could recite the recipes by heart. Georgina found them highlighted in neon pink marker in *The Fanny Farmer Cookbook* her mother gave her when she married Geoff: *Eggs Benedict, Boeuf Bourguignonne, Ratatouille Nicoise, Crepes, Chicken Timbales*. And, on page 463, *Princeton Orange Cake*, which Constance baked for herself and Georgina every year on the birthday they shared.

"Princeton," her mother would sigh after she finished reciting all of the ingredients in the cake and the method by which to prepare it, her ritual before she helped Georgina blow out the candles. "I should have gone to university. I should have been a scholar."

Although Georgina did not think Constance was especially curious or imaginative, her mother did love facts. She memorized encyclopedic tracts and the definitions of words she'd heard at work and didn't know the meaning of. She walked around the house while waiting for supper, repeating over and over the exact words from, say, the *Book of Knowledge, Volume 4*, or *The Concise Oxford Dictionary*.

"Cataract," Constance droned. "Noun. Waterfall (prop. large and sheer, cf cascade); downpour of rain, rush of water; (Path.) eye-complaint producing partial blindness; (Mech.) steam-engine governor acting by flow of water." She'd read the definition, every notation just as it appeared on the page, until she could repeat it word for word. *"The Concise Oxford Dictionary,"* she'd say once she got it right, then snap the book shut tight.

*

Constance has come to the office, ASAP, because Georgina asked her to. She tried to warn her, to tell her mother the details of the ultrasound and endoscopy report, but her mother refused to listen.

"Stop. Stop. My ears are plugged," Constance yelled into the telephone, "You're not my doctor. You don't know everything."

Georgina could hear the fear alongside the insult. Her mother wanted Karl, Dr. Malik, to tell her face to face what was wrong.

"If it's bad news, Georgina, I don't want to remember it coming from you," Constance added.

What Karl is going to tell Constance is that her lack of energy and occasional lower abdominal discomfort is really a 3 cm long cancer in her bowel. He'll tell her that he is sending her to a fine surgeon, the very best in the field, that the prognosis is good because the cancer is localized, that there are yards of bowel and taking a section will not be so bad. He'll tell her to come into the office whenever she feels the need for information or a talk, knowing she won't come. Once a specialist takes over it is a while before a patient comes back to see their family doctor. That's just the way it is.

And Georgina is just as happy she won't have to treat her mother during her ordeal. Somebody else will greet her at their office. Somebody else will test her urine, give her her shots, book her appointments. Georgina has her hands full being her mother's daughter.

Now here she stands, erect and severe, her eyes begging the information she has forbidden Georgina to share. When she decided to switch physicians and make Karl her family doctor, she asked Georgina to be strictly, excessively professional, and, as always, Georgina complies.

"We're going to go to the Elvis Presley Museum," her mother says.

"What?"

"Your father and I, when we go to Niagara Falls."

Georgina's parents went to Niagara Falls for their honeymoon in 1950, a trip her mother continues to talk about, a high point in her life. Never before her honeymoon, and never since, has she travelled further than the 582 kilometres to Niagara Falls.

While her parents were there, Red Hill Jr. went over the Falls in an impractical contraption made of inner tubes and fish net that he called "The Thing." They watched him die, then they stayed and watched as the river was dragged for Red's body. They saw parts of his contraption bob to the surface, joined the collective "Oh" of the two hundred thousand spectators.

It is the kind of drama her mother loves, the kind she'll never forget, wishes for, waits for, every single remaining day of her life.

Meanwhile she memorizes facts, tells anyone who will listen: Horseshoe Falls is 185 feet high, the plunge pool 180 feet deep. One hundred thousand cubic feet of water per second pass over the crestline during daylight in peak season times, half that amount in the off season and at nights, the rest diverted for hydro electric purposes. Georgina's parents are going for a second honeymoon for their forty-sixth wedding anniversary, a gift from Constance to her husband.

"Your father is going to find the barber who cut his hair the afternoon of our wedding, the day Red Hill Jr. drowned," her mother says as she touches her own angled pale hair. "It cost him ten dollars. A lot of money in those days, but the barber cut Frank Sinatra's hair, had his autographed picture on the wall, so the money was worth it. I sat and watched the whole thing, maybe from the chair Frank's girlfriend sat in, or Frank himself while he was waiting his turn. I should have asked. It was so exciting."

"I remember that story, Constance," Georgina reminds her mother. She particularly remembers the part where Red Jr.'s mother was heard to shout, *I want him back! I want him back*! just as he was going over the falls. The next day his broken body was recovered near the landing dock of the *Maid of the Mist*.

"We're getting a suite in the same hotel we stayed in in '50. It's a theme hotel now. Safari Room. Polar Room. Our room has a round bed and plants and vines, a leopard skin bedspread and lots of mirrors." Georgina whistles and rolls her eyes. "And we'll go to see the Falls at night. The lights on the spray, Georgina, my god they're the prettiest thing I've ever seen."

Georgina smiles harder, bigger, "I should take Geoff, what do you think? We could use a little romance." But the phone rings and Georgina is almost released.

"Lunch," her mother mouths and Georgina nods her head, "Yes."

Constance sits beside Francie Leblanc who is also waiting for Karl. Francie has lank brown hair and a hard little frosted pink mouth with tiny blazing white serrated teeth set as straight as dentures in her gums. When she smiles at Constance, Francie looks feral, and even thinner and smaller than her ninety-two pound, five-feet-nothing frame.

Francie has come because she got a death threat from her brother between 8 and 9 on Tuesday morning. "I want Dr. Malik to record it," she told Georgina when she booked the appointment, "I want it to be official, in black and white, just in case."

Francie comes in every other week to tell Karl about her past, lately about the naughty touches from years ago that Francie's brother told her never to speak about. Francie calls Georgina once a week to ask her to write something or other on her file so she won't forget to tell the doctor.

Karl calls Francie's name. Next it will be her mother's turn.

*

When she goes home Georgina will forget Francie and the other patients. Their names, their pain and joy. And today she will forget faster because she is making a twentieth birthday for Christopher: picking up a cake, wrapping presents, thinking of the right words to put on the card, grilling a steak.

What Georgina won't be able to forget is the look on her mother's face when she came out of Karl's office. Pale as her hair, stiletto lines slicing downward, thinning her, deflating her, as though the air had been pressed out of her body.

At lunch they talked about treatments and procedures. And how to tell Georgina's father, her mother's eyes misting over then, but when Georgina reached out to take her hand, her mother pulled it away and picked up a spoon. The surgery had been scheduled for a Thursday in three weeks' time. Her parents were supposed to leave for Niagara Falls on the weekend.

"Go. It will take your mind off things. You'll be relaxed when you get back. And it will be awhile before you'll be able to go again, especially if they decide to do radiation or chemo," Georgina advised.

Her mother watched her soup as she stirred it with her spoon, round and round forming a whirlpool of tomato broth with bits of carrot and celery surfacing, swirling in the vortex, disappearing.

"I don't want to talk about it," she said.

She turned away from Georgina and began to speak. Georgina leaned toward her mother.

"Did I ever tell you about Annie Edson Taylor? October 21, 1901. She was sixty-one but she lied and told the press she was only forty-two. She was teaching dancing and wasn't getting enough customers to make a living. She figured it was better to risk the Falls in a barrel than to continue living in poverty. Some people thought she was trying to commit suicide, but she told them she was too good an Episcopalian for that. It only took ten seconds. When they opened the lid of the barrel she heard someone ask, *Is the woman alive? Yes, she is!* Annie shouted, then she asked, *Did I go over the Falls?* It's a mystery, Georgina, what will kill you and what won't."

Constance sighed and turned toward Georgina. She pushed her soup away, "I'll call tonight to wish Christopher happy birthday."

*

When Malcolm was born, fifteen months after Christopher, Georgina felt the same as during her first labour. The only difference was that Malcolm was born after four hours, Christopher after twenty-eight.

"I'm an ordinary woman," she told anyone who asked, "simple and direct. I've broken some rules, but followed most of them. But when the contractions started I knew right away there were no rules: none to break and none to follow. I had to become the pain."

She told how giving birth was the only time in her life that she felt she was herself, Georgina Voll. That she never felt so alive. When her labour first began, she was overpowered by the force of the will of her body, but when she gave into the contractions, stopped resisting them, let them draw her to the brink, then over, she knew exactly who and what she was, what she had to do. She felt exactly right. There was only the pulsing, cascading rhythm of pain. And this one thing to be done. Push her baby out.

*

Karl Malik was her doctor when Christopher and Malcolm were born. The day Georgina brought Malcolm in for his starting school check-up Karl offered her the nurse's job. It was a big decision, for she had been an at-home mother since Christopher was born. She nursed the boys until they were ready to stop: Christopher when he was three and a half, Malcolm when he was almost four. She had opted for cloth diapers, which she washed herself. She prepared her own baby food, freezing it in ice cube trays: blended carrots, organic stewed puréed apricots, sieved rice and beans when they were older.

"Why do you go to all the trouble?" her mother once asked. "You could use disposables and buy prepared food. Why must you do this, Georgina?" Georgina hadn't bothered to answer.

But she did decide to take the job. She's been doing it now for thirteen years.

The door opens. Georgina doesn't look up this time. She knows who has arrived. She's that organized, writes down each appointment in the book, asks why each person is coming, pulls the files and makes sure they are up to date, that Karl has everything he needs to satisfy his patients.

This time it is Janet Barry come with her forty-two-year-old schizophrenic daughter, Sandra. Sandra is coming down from a quick love affair with a so-called artist and now that the love-high is passing, she needs her Fluanxol. When Sandra is in love she refuses all medication, help or advice. When Janet called to make the appointment she told Georgina that these affairs always ended badly. "She doesn't fall for the right sort of man," she said, "and it always ends in disaster."

Sandra is dishevelled, overweight, a little manic. She has an unlit cigarette in her mouth, practically chews on the filter. Every time she tries to light it her mother takes her hand, tells her to wait until they are out of the building. She glowers at her mother, but she waits. She flicks her lighter over and over and over.

"Thanks for fitting us in, Georgina," Janet says, as Georgina gives Sandra her injection. Janet's smile is rueful, Georgina's restrained. Georgina can't imagine having to look after a forty-two-year-old child.

When the phone rings Georgina isn't surprised that it's her mother.

"When is my appointment with the surgeon, Georgina?" she asks, "I forgot to write it down. Your father cried. And could you make a copy of all the reports. I'm making a file."

"We're not going to the Falls. We want to stay home, do some research, collect ourselves. But if we were going we'd get a holy relic, a piece of hawthorn from around Fort George. The missionaries brought hawthorn bushes grown from the original bush at Golgotha. Did you know that, Georgina? The one they used to make the crown of thorns for Jesus. And here I quote, '... *a study says the thorns are an Old World species that can be found growing nowhere else in North America,*' unquote."

*

As the boys stop needing her, as they begin to build their own lives, to have secrets, to have girlfriends whose bodies they must be exploring she thinks, Georgina has started to watch herself in mirrors, tries to see who is looking back. She wonders if Christopher and Malcolm ever think of her as having a body, or if she is so familiar as to be invisible to them, a presence yes, but myopically undefined. She watches parts of herself emerge changed: rounder, fuller, less angular and definite.

Shiny reflecting surfaces attract her and she remembers this curiosity from when she was a teenager, amorphous, just becoming aware of her presence, her physical being: breasts, hair, hips, eyes and mouth, belly, buttocks, knees, ankles, feet. Swirling disconnected parts.

*

Lately, Georgina feels pain, but not the same as when she was in labour. Sorrow. A constricting wad of it in her chest. When she gets home from work she takes off her shoes, lies down on the couch and thinks about Christopher and Malcolm. Thinks about her mother.

She cries. Great washes of tears stream right into her ears, overflow onto the cushions. Her nose runs and she lets it. She does not move until she hears the dog bark, her warning that someone is coming into the yard. Then she rushes upstairs, washes her face, blows her nose and gets on with it. Supper, conversation, newspaper, phone calls, a video sometimes, a book, maybe a game of cribbage since they cancelled the cable. The late news, lovemaking.

During lovemaking Georgina's body seems to separate from herself. She cannot imagine that sex was ever connected to making babies. Geoff was "fixed" right after they had Malcolm. Since then sex has always been safe, supposedly always for pleasure.

Georgina feels arousal, the ache of wanting, a fullness in her groin, Geoff's fingers and tongue on her breasts. But inside the cavity of her chest where her heart beats, waiting tears press and press. Press hard up against her throat, choking her. The tears release, finally, painfully, at the very moment her orgasm lifts her pelvis from the bed.

After Geoff falls asleep, Georgina gets up and lies down on the couch again, continues where she left off. When she is exhausted she goes back to bed. Often she is still up when Christopher or Malcolm come home from a late night out. Georgina cries so quietly that they do not notice her in the dark. Sometimes she is awake at dawn when the nesting cardinal and her mate whistle and trill back forth to each other, awake when the rest of the street awakens and the cardinals become silent.

*

Once Georgina called her mother, who slept less and less as she got older, she often complained. Constance said she listened to books-on-tape in the dark, turned her chair to face an east window where she watched silvery light filter into the black sky, watched silhouettes emerge from relief.

Georgina told her mother how sad she'd become whenever she thought about Christopher and Malcolm, that she'd tried so hard but now she sometimes wondered if she might have failed them. How they'd become distant and remote, so private, filled with secrets they no longer shared with her. She knew it was time to let them go, but it made her feel so lonely to think of them leaving.

"What goes around, comes around," her mother'd told her. "You were a wild one. You never listened to a word I said. You took off out west with that dope-dealing truck driver when you were eighteen and we didn't hear from you for a year."

Georgina had to laugh out loud, couldn't help it, for she remembered the truck driver, Kenny Stone, fine-boned, wavy dark hair everywhere, funny in bed, but lazy and often cruel. She'd smoked dope, dropped acid and collected welfare until she got a job as an nurse's aide on a paediatric oncology ward. A job she left a week before she left Kenny Stone lying in bed on a drizzly Monday morning in September, rubbing the curling hair around his navel, yelling, "Bitch, I don't fucking need you." On exactly the same day she entered university on a student loan to study nursing. Only then did she call her parents to tell them she was fine, that she'd got her act together.

"Yes, Georgina," her mother repeated, "What goes around, comes around."

*

Georgina closes and locks the door as Janet and Sandra leave. Sandra's cigarette smoke drifts in on the hallway draft. It smells so good sometimes, that first fresh exhalation of smoke. It reminds Georgina of summer nights, cars with windows open, bars. (And boys with bodies like gods, her own so thin and smooth and desirable.)

Tempting to start again. Georgina hasn't smoked since she decided to try to get pregnant with Christopher, which she succeeded in doing right after she went off the pill.

Both Christopher and Malcolm smoke. She can't figure it out. Geoff doesn't smoke, and they never allowed smoking in the house. The boys went to schools which were preachy, almost fascist, about a healthy safe lifestyle — good food, proper rest, exercise, no cigarettes, no drugs, no alcohol, no unprotected sex. The "no's" are the things her sons now love to do the most, she's sure.

Sadness is surfacing. If Georgina doesn't get out of the office soon the tears will start before she makes it home to the couch. Lately she finds it harder to confine herself to crying only when she is alone. This will pass, she tries telling herself, for how could she go on crying like this forever. But for now the tears come in movie theatres, concerts, once at the grocery store when she walked past a mother scolding her baby, and once when she was swimming, which, if she hadn't felt so miserable, would have been an interesting experience — tears in the water.

*

Georgina does remember a different kind of pain that made her cry and didn't last. Guilt. She had sex with Karl right there on the moss-green rug in his office. It had been coming for over a year that was filled with sexual tension and glances, the brushing of skin on skin. Once started, the real thing with tongues and kisses and clothes coming off, Georgina knew it was wrong and hated herself for being so weak and self-indulgent. But she didn't stop. She was crying before they were finished. Karl lay beside her, his pants around his ankles and licked the tears away; then he stood up and put his clothes back on.

Georgina had her back to Karl as she dressed and told him how she wanted this job, how she liked working for him — liked him — but she wouldn't allow this to happen again and if that was a problem for Karl he should say so right now. Karl said, "Whatever you think is best, Georgina."

They never mentioned it, though the tension, both arousal and guilt, remained for a long time. Georgina cried off and on when she felt remorse. Or terror. What if Geoff found out? What if he left her? What if he told Christopher and Malcolm?

That was years ago, but there are still times when Georgina calmly wonders what might have happened if she had decided to keep on making love to Karl, what her life would be like now. And she feels a particular dark pleasure, a wicked and nasty delight, from knowing that her mother occasionally stands, her long thin feet so confidently planted, on the very spot where she and Karl had made love.

*

Not all of Karl's patients are a sorry lot. The pregnant women, especially the first-time mothers, are optimistic and magnificent. Georgina thinks there should be a special place for them to wait, one filled with mirrors to reflect their beauty and radiance. Even Eadie Bester, who has eleven children, the last of which *came out in my pants*, looks more healthy and seems more confident when she is pregnant. The older mothers look youthful and vibrant, the younger ones so sure and graceful, their bodies just as they should be.

After the babies are born the mothers return for their babies' shots; for reassurance for themselves. Georgina oh's and ah's, tells the older mothers that theirs is the loveliest, fattest, sweetest, smartest baby she has ever seen. That they must be doing all the right things.

The youngest mothers, the ones in their teens and very early twenties want to hear that *they* are the ones who look lovely and sweet, that they are losing weight so quickly, that their hair is getting glossy and thick again. They still want to be the centre of attention. Once Georgina has complimented them, she can concentrate on their babies.

*

One afternoon, while Georgina lay crying on the couch, Malcolm arrived from nowhere. He had stayed home from school, he said, had been in his room. He didn't seem to notice Georgina's crying, at least didn't acknowledge it. "I wish I'd never been born," he hissed as he flopped down on the couch opposite Georgina's.

He told Georgina that she nagged him too much. He said he was going through a hard time and he didn't need her telling him about jobs and marks and helping out all the time. When Georgina asked him what he was finding difficult and could she help, he yelled, "See there you go again, always butting in. Just leave me alone. Stop nagging," and he got up and stomped out of the room.

*

Georgina buys wrapping paper and a birthday card decorated with electric guitars. Christopher's favourite pastime is playing guitar though Georgina has noticed he doesn't play as much as he used to. She picks up the cake in the shape of a guitar at the bakery. She and Geoff bought Christopher an electric guitar tuner, an array of new picks, new strings for the Gibson Les Paul (cherry starburst pattern) Christopher bought with his first pay cheque after he quit high school two years ago.

Georgina buys the steak Christopher asked her to cook for his birthday supper, the new potatoes, salad greens, red onions for frying. She rushes home to get them ready.

*

These days, Georgina doesn't have to worry about Christopher finding her on the couch crying. He comes home only occasionally, and though lately he is often gentle and sweet, as though he too knows he will soon be gone forever, he just as often rants about the stupidity of a world that doesn't treat him fairly and the faults of a mother who doesn't understand.

He comes to do a laundry, to pick up fresh clothes, borrow five dollars, to make a meal. He leaves the mess, says he'll clean it up when Georgina asks him to, but when he is gone the dirty dishes, smears of sauce, cheese, crumbs, splashes of milk and juice remain, a still-life of his chaos, and of his disregard.

Georgina dreads the times when her friends talk about their children. Sometimes, instead of crying, Georgina thinks up answers to, "What are Christopher and Malcolm doing these days?"

"Studying in Geneva, then travelling to Antarctica," she once said. "Just kidding," she quickly added when the reply was taken seriously.

Dealing blackjack. Following a rock band from town to town, concert to concert. Learning the intricacies of marijuana cultivation. Fucking a great deal. Joining a circus. Exotic dancing. She doesn't know. If they are doing something they aren't telling her.

Georgina also listens for the telltale signs of discord in her friends' conversations. Jenny is at Concordia but doesn't like academics. (What does that mean, Georgina wants to ask. How can you be at university and not like academics? But she knows the answer will be oblique or deferred). Shaun had to be sent money two weeks after he got his student loan, but he is making lots of lovely friends and is getting around Montreal so well. Michael has a new girlfriend who has two toddlers and seems to be a nice woman. He is getting through second year at Queen's though he is seldom in his room when his mother calls.

It is the unsaid that fascinates Georgina. All that is under the surface. But even this makes her cry, this possible failing of children who are not even her own.

*

When Georgina gets home there is a message on the answering machine from her mother, "Hello? Hello? Georgina are you there? It's Constance. Georgina? I hate machines. I won't call anymore if it's a machine. We're better now, but your father has some questions for you about this cancer. Call him."

Her tone changes, warming up, "Oh, and Georgina, I was just telling your father about Jerome Bonaparte. You know, Napoleon's brother. He was the first famous honeymooner at Niagara Falls. He married a woman from Baltimore, Maryland, but the marriage didn't last, not like your father's and mine. Your father says we can go to Niagara next year. 'We'll go to Niagara next year, Constance,' he said in that big deep voice of his. He's like you, such an optimist." Then there is a click and the sound of a dial tone before the machines begins to rewind.

As Georgina cleans potatoes, Christopher calls. His friends are taking him out for supper, he says; he won't be home. No, he probably won't stop by later as they are going to a bar afterwards.

"Christopher," Georgina protests.

"'Bye, Mom. I'll wake you up when I get home."

"Happy birthday," she says, but he has already hung up.

The phone rings again.

"Georgina, it's Constance, is Christopher there?"

Georgina tells her that Christopher is out celebrating with friends.

"What? I thought you said you were cooking him steak?"

"I was."

"You shouldn't let him walk all over you. Don't be a doormat for your kids. Tough love, that's what they need."

"We've decided to give you our trip to Niagara. The room is already paid for and we booked ahead on the *Maid of the Mist*. I think you're looking a little ragged these days, Georgina. You could use a rest. Take Geoff."

"And be sure to go to the Floral Clock. I was just reading that there are 19,000 plants used every year in the Floral Clock. Isn't that something. Tell Christopher I called. Tell him I'd like to speak to him before I die."

"You're not going to die."

"Oh yes I am. Maybe not now, but I will surely die. Goodbye, Georgina."

*

Georgina stumbles to the couch, falls on it. She is choked with sorrow, a stinging urgent press of uncried tears. She shudders. Wracking spasms, one, then another and another, shoot up and down her body. Her muscles knot. Pain stabs her calves, slashes her thighs, crashes across her shoulders. Sluices down into her wrists. Into her hands and fingers.

Georgina screams.

She screams and cries and screams.

Then suddenly she is laughing. Painfully — rasping and hard — but purely. Wildly. Laughing.

She gets up and gathers some of the birthday preparations, puts them on a tray and carries it to her bedroom. She lifts the covers from her bed, lays out her surprises one by one on her crisp clean sheets — cake, potatoes, salad, fried onions. She lies down, pulls a blanket around her, flicks on the TV and begins to eat with her fingers, wiping them occasionally on Geoff's pillow. She does not get up when she hears the dog's warning bark.

*

When her mother and father went on their honeymoon to Niagara Falls, her mother was eighteen, her father twenty. Her mother's period started as they checked into the hotel. Constance liked to tell how Georgina's father had to go out to a drugstore in his wedding suit and buy Kotex for his bride. As he was coming back up to her on the elevator, which was crowded with people, the bag ripped and there he stood, a young man with confetti in his hair holding a box of Kotex. A groom who was definitely not getting any that night.

Georgina thought that Constance liked to tell this story to embarrass her, to remind her that she knew about the dark and intimate parts of Georgina's body. And that in this profound and inescapable way, they were, mother and daughter, alike.

The second part of the Niagara Falls story Georgina figured out herself. Nine months and two weeks from their wedding day, on her mother's nineteenth birthday, Georgina was born.

*

Georgina eats salad with her fingers; oil drips down her chin. She knows what she's going to do. She's going to Niagara Falls. Alone.

She'll walk along the edge of the Falls at night, see the lights on the water and in the spray. Take the room with the round bed and the leopard skin bedspread, the one with all the mirrors to piece together and watch the parts of her surprising, ever-changing body.

She'll ride the *Maid of the Mist* in a yellow slicker and sou'wester with tourists and honeymooners with confetti in their hair; visit Louis Tussaud's Museum, Marineland, the Criminal's Hall of Fame. She'll find the barber who cut Frank Sinatra's hair, and ask him to give her a trim, no expense spared. Look into the corners of the room to see if the shadow of her mother lingers there. Leave a big tip.

She'll ride the Spanish Aero Car above the Whirlpool, watch for a woman named Annie to sweep by in a barrel. Later she'll search the bushes around Fort George for hawthorn relics, tape bits of woody stem to postcards and mail them to her mother, and to her sons.

And if she must Georgina will weep. She will let her tears become the whirling, the constant churning water that crashes over that ancient and slowly eroding cliff.

About the Contributors

GABRIELLA GOLIGER is co-winner of the 1997 Journey Prize for short fiction and was a finalist for this prize in 1995. She also won the Prism International Short Fiction Contest in 1993. Her work has been published in *Parchment: Contemporary Canadian Jewish Writing*, *Canadian Forum* and *Tide Lines: Stories of Change by Lesbians*. Three of her stories will be featured in the 1998 edition of *Coming Attractions* published by Oberon Press. A child of escapees from the Holocaust, she was born in Merano, Italy, and has lived in Canada and Israel. She is working on a story collection, *Wanderers*, which draws on her background as an immigrant of German-Jewish heritage and explores themes such as relationship to place, history and family.

Photo credit: Photo of the painting *Zoë and Me, Number Four* by Esther Schvan; year 1996-1997; size 24" X 30"; medium: acrylic on canvas. ESTHER SCHVAN was born in Vienna, Austria, and is the daughter of Holocaust survivors. She lived in England and Israel before settling down in Canada in 1986. She was drawn to art early in life and has studied at various art institutions since 1977, but only began painting five years ago. Her first attempts led to an outpouring of creativity — vibrant expressions in acrylic on canvas that won acclaim at numerous exhibitions in Ottawa and which are hanging in private collections in Europe and Canada. Her paintings explore relationships with family and friends, particularly her own troubled childhood and her experiences as a mother of a special needs child.

SHARON HAWKINS lives in Ottawa where she works in children's mental health services. She has published in several literary magazines including *Arc*, *Room of One's Own*, *Fireweed* and *CVII*. She is an associate editor of *Arc* magazine and is completing her first manuscript. Some of the poems in "Preserving Jars" have appeared previously: "A Woman is Drawing Her Mother" (*Arc*); "Geraniums", "Gestures", and "Winter Solstice I" (*Room of One's Own*); "Something About Renewal" and "Tomato Marmalade" (*Fireweed*).

Photo credit: *Preserving Jars* photo taken by MARC ANDRE VACHON of Ottawa.

NADINE McINNIS is the author of three books of poetry: *Shaking the Dreamland Tree, The Litmus Body* and *Hand to Hand* and one book of literary criticism, *Poetics of Desire*, on the love poems of Dorothy Livesay. Her poetry has received several awards including First Prize in the National Poetry Contest of the League of Canadian Poets, Second Prize in the CBC Literary Competition and the Ottawa-Carleton Book Award. Her stories have appeared in the 1997 *Coming Attractions*, edited by Maggie Helwig, in *Vital Signs: New Women Writers*, edited by Diane Schoemperlen and in *The Malahat Review, Quarry, Windsor Review* and *Event*. Her stories won first prize in both the 1993 and 1996 Nepean Library Short Story Contest. Nadine wishes to acknowledge William Langewieshe's travel writing, especially *Sahara Unveiled: A Journey Across the Desert* (Pantheon, 1996).

Photo credit: BILL KRESOWATY, 1998. This photo was taken for this story close to the imagined setting, near Bright Sand Lake, Saskatchewan.

SANDRA NICHOLLS' first book, *The Untidy Bride*, was short-listed for the Pat Lowther Award in 1991. Her second book of poems, *Women of Sticks, Women of Stones*, won the Archibald Lampman Award for Poetry in 1998. She also received third prize in the International Stephen Leacock Poetry Awards in 1994. She currently lives in Ottawa where she works as a freelance writer and editor.

Photo credit: *The Bone Fields, 1992* by DAN STEEVES; crayon etching,8/16; support size: 56.5 x 76 cm; plate size: 45.3 x 60.7 cm; Collection of the Owens Art Gallery

SUSAN ZETTELL lives in Ottawa. Her stories have appeared in *The University of Windsor Review, The Capilano Review, Canadian Forum* and other literary journals. Her first collection, *Holy Days of Obligation*, is to be published in the fall of 1998 by Nuage Editions. She is also co-editor, with Frances Itani, of *One of the Chosen*, a posthumous collection of short stories by Danuta Gleed.

Photo credit: photo by ANDY WATT, 1977.

ABOUT THE EDITOR

RITA DONOVAN was born in Montreal. She has published five novels: *River Sky Summer* (ITP Nelson, 1998), *The Plague Saint* (Tesseract Books, 1997), *Landed* (BuschekBooks, 1997), *Daisy Circus* (Cormorant Books, 1991) and *Dark Jewels* (Ragweed Press, 1990). She is co-editor of *Arc* (poetry) magazine, a freelance reviewer, editor and teacher. Rita has received the 1998 Canadian Authors Association/Chapters Award for fiction; she was a finalist for the W.H. Smith/Books in Canada First Novel Award in 1990 and she is twice winner of the Ottawa-Carleton Book Award (1991 and 1993). She lives in Ottawa with her husband and daughter.

Photo credit: cover photo *November* by ANNA MARIA CARLEVARIS; n.d.

EDITOR'S NOTE

A few years ago I attended a reading at a local Ottawa art gallery. Among those at the podium that night was Sharon Hawkins who presented several poems on the subject of mothers, daughters and grandmothers. Without fanfare she managed to tap into this powerful, pervasive bond, and I was very moved by her reading.

I realize, subsequently, that the poems never really left me. And as I spoke with other writers I knew, women who, like me, have mothers or children or both in our lives, I was surprised at how often our conversations about writing would slip into discussions of family concerns. I wondered how the lives of mothers and children might manifest themselves in the fiction and poetry of these writers. I asked the question and was overwhelmed with their response. *Quintet* is the result of the exploration of this first bond. Some of the children in this book are adults now, dealing with ageing parents and, perhaps, their growing children as well. Some of the children are young observers, warily making their way in the world. All of the voices speak of the unique and complicated balance of loss and gain that exists between mother and child.

Not all of the women in this collection are mothers. All are daughters, however, and all are writers, good writers. It has been extremely rewarding working with these talented women — Gabriella Goliger, Sharon Hawkins, Nadine McInnis, Sandra Nicholls and Susan Zettell. As for my part, what began as a simple question with the potential of becoming an interesting project has evolved into an absolute delight.

Rita Donovan